The Adventures of Hawke Travis

Center Point
Large Print

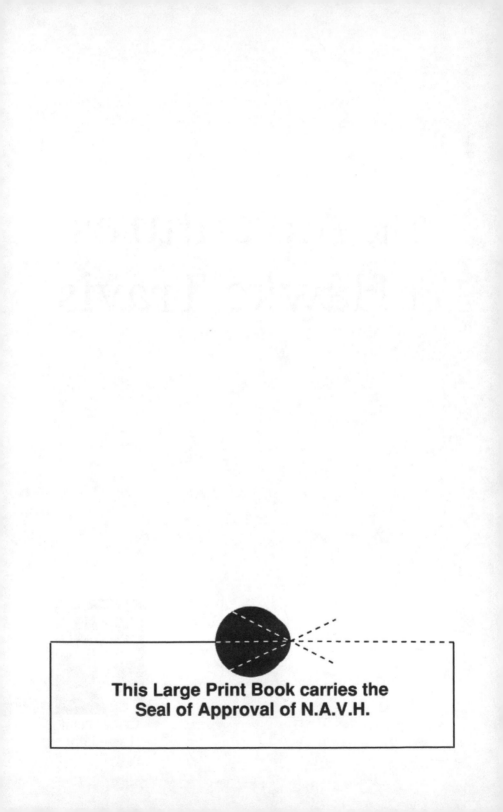

**This Large Print Book carries the
Seal of Approval of N.A.V.H.**

The
Adventures
of
Hawke Travis

Eli Colter

CENTER POINT LARGE PRINT
THORNDIKE, MAINE

This Center Point Large Print edition is published
in the year 2014 by arrangement with
Golden West Literary Agency.

The text of this Large Print edition is unabridged.
In other aspects, this book may vary
from the original edition.
Printed in the United States of America
on permanent paper.
Set in 16-point Times New Roman type.

ISBN: 978-1-62899-062-1

Library of Congress Cataloging-in-Publication Data

Colter, Eli.
 The adventures of Hawke Travis / Eli Colter. — Center Point Large Print
edition.
 pages ; cm
 ISBN 978-1-62899-062-1 (library binding : alk. paper)
 1. Large type books. I. Title.
 PS3505.O368A65 2014
 813'.52—dc23
                                                        2013048112

To
"HAWKE,"
who knows the meaning
of the word
friend.

I

Hawke Travis was one of the many aliases he wore at one time or another. Let it serve here. It isn't the name that is of vital interest, anyway; it is the man. Some scoffers would have us believe that the Old West, the West of "Blazing Six-guns and Magnificent Heroism," is a myth, a figment of the unbridled imaginations of the incurably romantic. Others—tongue in cheek and one eye about half closed—assert with fine and caustic irony that in the saga of the West it is, to the writers thereof, the musical clink of the dollar which lures; and will lure as long as avid youth, straining against inhibition and enforced prosaic surroundings, will spend its dimes to purchase the pulps which exploit fiction of that much mooted era.

To some extent both are correct. In a few quarters we give the scoffers right; simply because in the major number of instances the picture of the West has been distorted and ill presented. But—behind all the flub-dub and hokum, half-veiled by the lurid heterogeneties of the hyperbolists, looms that which is sought by that avid youth, the very real Old West. There were men of daring and exquisite proficiency, who were the prototypes of the exaggerated heroes who blaze through our melodramatic pulp Western fiction of today.

Hawke Travis was one of these. Today, he nears eighty years of age. He stands finely erect. His hair is quite white, but still a rough mass of curl. His eyes are as keen and black, his wit as sharp and ready, as both were fifty years ago. I know him as well as one human being usually knows another, for the simple reason that between us there has never existed any evasion. There was in the very moment of our meeting a sure understanding that has never been clouded, because it never knew any falsity.

To know Hawke Travis is to respect him, to like him. Personally, I love him sincerely. Not too many do. He is too without pretense, too nakedly Hawke Travis. Not a great number of us genuinely love a human soul unclothed by the habiliments of polite and lying social amenities.

But consider this. If Hawke should tell you a thing was true, you could safely wager your life on the veracity of that thing and know you would not lose. If Hawke should give you his word for a deed, to be performed next week or ten years hence, you could know the deed was as well as accomplished—unless Hawke should be in his grave before the hour of fulfillment should arrive. If Hawke should want to borrow from me any sum of money at all, and I should have it to lend, I would quite as quickly think of slapping him in the face as I would think of asking for his note. It would be an insult to his word. And—if I were in need of fifty dollars, and Hawke had but twenty-five, he would borrow the other twenty-five and pretend disgraceful affluence, declaring that necessity of repayment of the loan was a large jest, asserting carelessly that "there was more where that came from." Hawke Travis—today.

Hawke Travis, some fifty-odd years ago: not tall, little above average height, but with a slenderness and carriage which made him seem taller than he was. Very much tanned. Straight as a soldier. Black mass of curl for hair. Black penetrating eyes under heavy black brows. Drooping black mustache. Very handsome indeed. Important item—one heavy black gun, Colt, frontier model, worn inside the waistband of his trousers, in front. He never wore a belt. Though "Western" fiction seldom pictures the gunman minus the cartridge-filled, sagging, romantic belt, the fact remains that numerous gunmen used no belt. Holes used to wear in Hawke's vest where the cloth covered the protruding loading gate of the gun thrust under his waistband. He was the typical handsome, smooth, cool-brained gunman of the Old West.

He was born on the Western Reserve, in northeastern Ohio. His father was a "down-East" Yankee, who before going to Ohio, had been a fisherman sailing out of Bangor, Maine. He was, at the time Hawke—the first of seven children—was born, owner of a brickyard and a store in a small town south of Cleveland.

Hawke's mother was a member of a well-known family of Virginia. Since it is very necessary indeed that Hawke's identity remain unrevealed, her name does not enter here. I shall be forced at times to use a few fictitious names, and in all such cases I shall state that the name used is false, and give the reason for it. Hawke's mother's father was a Campbellite preacher and a prominent pioneer of that section of Ohio. She was of a literary turn of mind. She was graduated from Hiram College, where she was a classmate of the twentieth President of the United States, James A. Garfield.

She never realized her literary ambitions. After the birth of her first child, her family absorbed her time. From this beginning, then, from this family root, came the child who was to become one of the gunmen of the "wild and woolly West." He may have inherited a fondness for literature from his mother, to the extent at least that he became early in life an eager reader. He laid then the foundation for the careful speech that he never deserted. Expanding, avid for knowledge, he read everything that came his way. Beadle's Dime Novels held him a while, but he became disgusted with what he now terms the "impeccable and impossible heroes of those improbable tales." Then he turned to Scott, Dickens, Byron, and to the American authors of more than fifty years ago.

It was Dickinson's "Beyond the Mississippi" that fired him with the ambition to go West and become an Indian fighter or a trapper. When he was nine years old, his father sold out his business and moved to southeastern Kansas, in 1867. The country was full of wild game, and malaria. They were forty miles from the nearest railroad, the K. C., Fort Scott and Gulf. Hawke got little schooling there. He spent most of his time working on the farm and in hunting. The embryo gunman first became a good shot then with his Manhattan cap-and-ball revolver. The whole family, now two adults and six children, lived in a one-room log cabin with a sod roof and lean-to kitchen. That is not a fair memory for Hawke. He calls it "a sordid mess." There was only one bed in the house. Most of them slept on the floor. Things did not thrive. Stock died for lack of care and shelter. Crops went to ruin for lack of fences and proper tending. Fever and ague struck heavily at the health of, and sapped the ambition of, all of them.

But to Hawke, there was a dream of something better. The dream of running away to make his fortune in the West. But his parents sent him to an uncle in Iowa, where he worked in summer-time, and went to school in the winter. He crammed hard, he wanted so badly to learn. He secured a third-grade certificate. And the embryo gunman taught school for a winter term, in the country, at the wages of thirty dollars a month.

The next spring, the spring of 1877, the dream of the West would no longer be denied. With a chum, Hawke started for the Black Hills. They went on the train to Sioux Falls, or rather to within a few miles of the town at the falls of the James River. So, out of this background, with this start, one of the West's future gunmen came, across the plains with bull-team and covered wagon, into the Black Hills and on, over years and miles till we find him full-blown Hawke Travis of the devilish eyes, with the deadly gun resting inside his waistband.

It was in a small town in Idaho. The hour was evening, the month was June. Joe Towers was seated in a knife-scarred chair on the front veranda of the Overland Hotel. Joe Towers wore another name than this, but it might be that he would demur at seeing his name in print, did he ever chance to read this biography. So, here he shall be Joe Towers. As he sat there, the Nampa stage came to a halt in a cloud of dust raised by its own wheels. Joe's lips twisted into a grin and his eyes lighted as a dark slender man descended from the high front seat of the stage and drew a saddle and a war bag from the compartment under the seat known as the boot. As the dusty traveler lugged his belongings up the steps and onto the porch, Joe rose and thrust out a hand.

"Well, well, well!" he greeted the newcomer. "What won't a man see when he ain't got a gun!

Where in hell have you been, and who have you been doing?"

Hawke's face then, as always during that era, was almost as dark as an Indian's, and usually as inscrutable. He dropped his load and gripped the extended hand. There was nothing in his countenance to show any pleasure at this chance meeting with an old acquaintance, save the look that leaped to the black eyes.

"Why, I've been doing myself, Joe, more than anyone else." Hawke chuckled dryly as he took the adjoining chair and seated himself beside Towers. "I've had to drink too much alkali water. I've been over on the J Bar S, breaking a few wild ones. But alkali and catarrh of the head make a bad combination. I had to pull my freight. What's the good word with you? Why the sad look? Did you get a few pat hands topped last night?"

"Nope." Joe shook his head, and gloom clouded his face. "Wasn't sittin' in at all last night, Hawke. I didn't have the price. That rancher I've been working for *says* he hasn't got the money to pay my wages. Serves me right for going to work shovelin' hay, when I could have got a riding job if I'd rustled for it." Towers frowned, and it was quite apparent to Hawke that he was badly disgruntled about something. In that first moment of reunion with Hawke, his temper had been subdued, but now his irritation was coming to the surface swiftly. Hawke hazarded a guess that it was probably nothing more than having had to work several months for nothing. Enough, granted, to roil anyone.

"Why don't you sue him?" Hawke suggested. In the rambling experiences of the past several years, Hawke had acquired much diversified knowledge, not the least of it accruing from a period spent in a lawyer's office.

Towers snorted. "Sue hell!" He spat his disgust over the railing, his scowl darkening. "A poor man's got no business going to law with one that's well fixed. You ought to know that. They'd make me put up a bond for costs and keep staving off the trial. I'd rather go up against brace faro-bank. I reckon I'll do my own collecting after this."

Hawke grinned, but he shook his head in disapproval. "You'd be bound to get the worst of it. They'd nail you sure as guns if you went on the prod."

"Oh, they would?" Towers sneered openly. "Well, we'll see about that. Where you headin' for?"

Hawke shrugged. "Anywhere. Anywhere where the water's purer than it is in Boise Valley. That damned alkali caused my head to swell so badly that I had to go to a doctor. He told me to beat it. Damn the luck, I liked the valley. Made me mad. I'm still rearin'. Got a notion to go on the prod myself."

"Oh, so?" Towers shot a sharp look at him. "You

14

and me ought to make a pretty fair team, Hawke. Never knew each other none too well, but it's easy to remedy that."

Hawke merely looked at him, but the look was enough. Towers returned his intent gaze with a meaning smile. So, as lightly as that, two men of casual acquaintance and very hot temper, meeting by chance when each had grievance enough to inflame his hot temper, swore some kind of silent and reckless oath to go "on the prod" together. Joe Towers was infuriated because the rancher who had hired him was withholding from him the wages he had earned, pretending a poverty that was manifestly nonexistent. Hawke's ire was roused to a high pitch because the irritation in his head had driven him out of the valley he liked so well, just when he had almost decided to settle and cease his roaming. Odd, that. At the very hour of life when he contemplated that settling, his most hectic era was about to be born.

Towers leaned close to him, his voice lowered. "What do you say we drift for the Wind River country or Jackson's Hole? The water's fine in both places. It will cost us little, only for the grub we eat on the way."

"I'm not over-fond of walking," Hawke said dryly.

"Don't need to walk. I'll lift a couple of horses from the ranch. Get that much of the wages that's due me, anyway."

15

Hawke made no demur. What was a little thing such as "lifting" a horse or two? But he frowned, considering another angle of the situation. "How will I get my outfit away from here without tipping my hand?"

Towers grinned. "Who cares? Take your hull out and hide it in the brush east of town. If anyone sees you, they'll think you're heading for another ranch. I'll do the rest. I'll meet you on the Camas Prairie road about ten o'clock."

Hawke nodded silent agreement. From that day Hawke began to aid in building the saga of the Old West.

II

When Towers arrived at the rendezvous at the appointed time, he found Hawke waiting in the brush where they two had hidden their riding gear and a light camping outfit. Towers was leading a large roan horse, and a still larger bay gelding. In silence, and with expert dispatch, they prepared for the night ride, rolled up their belongings in their slickers and tied the slickers to the cantles of their saddles. Towers mounted the roan, leaving the big bay to Hawke. They took the trail to the east, traveling steadily, avoiding scattered ranches where dogs might bark in warning to sleeping masters, and did not stop until the dawn began to lighten the sky above the sage-green desert to the east. There they turned left into the foothills, and sought a secluded spot in which to pass the day, where they might be protected from the sun—and from pursuers. Hawke gathered dry aspen sticks for a fire, chanting softly to himself:

> "Oh, Saturday night I stole a hoss
> And Sunday I was taken,
> Monday was my trial day,
> And Friday hung my bacon."

Towers favored him with a dry smile, "Feelin' cocky, eh? But you'd better not holler till we're out of the woods. They hang a rustler in this country quicker than they do a killer. Of course you didn't know that."

Hawke winked. "Catching before hanging. They haven't nabbed us yet. They'll have to go some if they take me while I'm able to use old Betsy." Hawke's face twisted in a wry grimace as he patted the stock of the forty-four Colt in the waistband of his trousers.

Towers shook his head. "They'll give you no chance at that hog leg, even if you do know how to use it."

Hawke scowled in open pique. "Even if I do know how to use it? What do you take me for, a tenderfoot?"

It must be admitted that Hawke was decidedly touchy regarding his skill with that Frontier Colt. That Towers should be lacking in appreciation of his speed and finesse was not at all to his liking. He resolved abruptly to show Towers something of his gun mastery at the first opportunity. Hawke was a handsome man with a magnetic personality, and women had figured in his life and passed on. Nothing of this type affected Hawke's vanity, or caused it. But let any man express a doubt of his ability with a gun, and Hawke was pricked in a vulnerable place. Towers cut into his scowling musing.

"You see, Hawke, I took them horses out of the corral at the old guy's place in town. He generally keeps two or three of the best of his remuda there, to make long rides or drives with. And we can expect to have the sheriff after us as quick as the old geeser finds out his horses is gone."

Hawke stared. "Out of the corral? You darned fool! Why didn't you take them off the range?" Hawke's displeasure was not caused by the likelihood of immediate pursuit being occasioned by Joe's reckless act, but merely by the realization that it had been to some extent rather a dumb thing to do. Taking uselessly long chances, when a thing could be done so much more smoothly by taking less chance, smacked somewhat of stupidity. Stupidity irked Hawke. He prided himself on his finesse.

But Joe answered serenely, taking no offense: "There wasn't any out in the hills worth a whoop in hell. So I took them two out of the corral, leaving the bars partly down. Well, let's get busy. Ought to make the Wood River country before another morning."

Before sunrise of the next day they were camped in a secluded place within a mile of a town in the Wood River Valley. There they remained until nightfall, watching the grazing horses and guarding against surprise by pursuing officers, each relieving the other at watch. By now they were short of food. There was no timidity about Hawke. Almost invariably he chose the bold course. He chose it now. At his suggestion, the horses were moved up to within a quarter mile of the town and tethered there. Then the two men walked boldly into the town to find a restaurant and a meal. They had entered near the upper end of the main business street, well away from most of the saloons and other business places fronting the street. They felt comparatively safe as they entered the little restaurant and found seats. Hawke sat with his back to a wall, facing the front door. Out of the corner of his eye he caught sight of a man scrutinizing him and Towers through one of the front windows.

The meal had arrived and they had begun to eat. Not a muscle of Hawke's face moved. He glanced at Towers casually, and as casually remarked in a low tone: "Take a look out that left-hand front window, Joe. Be careful not to tip off your hand."

Towers looked, and suppressed a start. The man before the window wore a star. "What'll we do?" Towers whispered. "Duck out the back way?"

Hawke shook his head. "Try that, and you'll have the whole burg at your heels. Follow me, and you'll wear diamonds—or a ball and chain."

His black eyes gleamed with amusement. He figured this might be good. Leisurely he finished his coffee. He rose from his chair, secure in his nonchalance and poise, and strolled over to the counter to pay for the meal, his spur-chains jingling behind his high-heeled boots. Quite as nonchalantly and leisurely he strolled on toward the front door, his right hand thrust into the outside pocket of his coat. As Hawke started to pass the man by the window, the officer stepped squarely into the path of Towers and Travis, his eyes on Joe.

"Just a minute, pardner. Are you the fellow who goes by the name of Joe Towers?"

"That's what the law sharks would call a leading question," Hawke cut in, before Joe could reply. "Such questions are barred in court, also here. Take your hand away from that gun!" Hawke's black eyes hardened and he thrust forward suggestively the hand in his coat pocket. "Now, turn around, round that next corner, and keep going down the side street. Don't try any smooth work. I'll be right behind you."

The officer scowled and cast a quick glance about him. No one was near. At this hour the street was quite deserted. He hesitated a split second, shot a glance at the position of Hawke's threatening hand, and obeyed the order. They encountered no one as they left the town, emerging from the short side street and hurrying into the brush where the fugitives had left the two horses. The officer frowned at the animals and then at Hawke.

"I must say, you're a cool one." Hawke made no reply, but disarmed him in silence. The officer demanded irritably: "Well, what do you damned horse thieves aim to do with me now? You wouldn't have got the edge on me so easily if I'd been sure you were the fellows I was looking for."

"Think so?" Hawke's grin was exasperating. "Well, we're not going to hurt you any, just take you for a little stroll down the gulch. Will you be good, or are you going to force me to jam a handkerchief into your mouth or bend a gun over your head?"

The officer swore to relieve his chagrin. "Do I look like a fool?"

Much of the officer's ire was appeased when they finally halted some two miles below the town. He had noted a few things. Hawke had made no further move to threaten him. He had not swung on his horse and left only the officer to walk. The three had walked together, leading the horses. When they stopped, Hawke returned the officer's Colt, empty.

The man laughed. "Damned if you aren't more than half white, if you are rustlers. Too white to be cut off at the pockets or to stretch rope—or to be stealing horses."

Hawke grinned again. "Well, we had a long journey to make, and we're none too fond of walking. I'll wager that, by the time you get back to town, you'll feel like agreeing that it's no fun."

"You're a devil, young man!" the officer snapped. "But let me give you a tip. Your time's short in this vale of tears. The sheriff sent me a wire from Boise to be on the lookout for you. The whole Wood River country will be on your trail as quick as I can get back to town and notify deputy sheriff Carson that you've showed up here. So long. Be good and you'll be happy." And the officer waved a hand as he turned to retrace his steps.

Towers and Travis rode rapidly down-river. Evidently the sheriff at Boise had in some manner learned that they had traveled east, and had acted accordingly, had telegraphed to all the towns along the Oregon Short Line to the south to be on the lookout for the two men.

"We'd better turn east again and keep away from the railroad, Hawke," Towers suggested. "We'd better keep to the trail between the lava beds and the Sawtooth Range, so we can dodge into the mountains if we have to."

Hawke nodded silent approval. Towers knew this country much better than he. Realizing that there would be little chance to conceal their trail from the pursuing posse that would be tracking them, Travis and Towers rode their mounts hard. They continued to ride on through the night, not even stopping to eat. They contented themselves with a little cooked food from their saddlebags. Dawn found them at the Crossing of Lost River, which stream was still unusually high because of the melting snow in the Sawtooth Range. There they paused to survey the roiled waters rushing over their steep and rocky bed with the force of a millrace. Hawke remarked that the crossing was dangerous.

Towers informed him that here was the only ford for four miles. Above, the water was worse; below, the river spread over the lava beds and there was danger of quicksand. There was only one thing to do; that was, to try to cross here. They forced the reluctant horses to enter the cold, turbulent stream and fight their way to the other side. The waters were so swift that the two animals finally brought their riders to a landing a good hundred yards below. Towers grunted in satisfaction, and turned to Travis with some explanation.

"That'll help some, Hawke. We've got to make a long detour around the store at the Crossing. The old man that runs it is death on horse thieves, and also is the leader of the Vigilantes organized to put the kibosh on the gangs that have been operating around here. He'd make short work of us if he could lay hands on us. But, we've got to eat. I'm hollow to the toes."

"Oh, we'll eat," Hawke assured him confidently.

Towers instantly divined what Hawke had in mind, as they left the river behind. Jackrabbits were plentiful in the sage-brush country through which they were riding. He protested quickly. "But we won't dare build any fire to roast any jackrabbits, Hawke. Besides, they're mighty poor eating at this time of year. And another besides, how do you expect to get one of them damn things with a six-shooter?"

"A fire will be no give-away if we use dead aspen and don't make it too big," Hawke returned. "I'd rather eat prairie dog than risk going to any of the ranches around here for grub. As for getting the rabbits—" Hawke shrugged. Joe was the fellow who had made a disparaging hint concerning his ability with a Colt. The pricked vanity of the gunman nudged him as a rabbit leaped out of the sage. The Colt forty-four jerked out of Hawke's waistband, cracked at the behest of Hawke's finger; the rabbit leaped into the air and flopped to the ground. Towers stared.

"Was that just a happen-so?" he demanded. Hawke denied vehemently that the evidence of his excellent marksmanship was any "happen-so." To prove it, he shot two more of the fleet-limbed rabbits frightened out of the sage by the horses. Towers shook his head wonderingly. "Where in the name of God did you ever learn to shoot like that?"

Hawke's piqued vanity was appeased. "I'm Deadwood Dick, the bad, bad man from Bitter Crick," he retorted, as he ejected an empty shell from his gun; but his innate honesty prodded him to add, "It's nothing. I used to shoot prairie chickens on the wing back in Kansas, and I've been practicing with a six-gun ever since I was old enough to own one. You see, from the time I was knee-high to a hop-toad, I always dreamed of going West. I'd made up my mind I'd practice till those Western bad men would have no edge on me. And I guess I did and they haven't."

Usually, nay, always, if a man dreams about a thing and adheres to it long enough, he can make his dream reality. Hawke's dream had already begun to mature, had he but known it. The two of them gathered up the three rabbits, then turned to the northeast, keeping to a rocky dry wash leftward from the main trail, and within a half hour were camped in a park-like spot high up in the foothills, and nearly a mile to the north of the road between the lava beds and the mountains. There they made their meal, and took stock of their situation.

They were badly in need of sleep, as men a few jumps ahead of a posse and a rope often are. They decided they could safely sleep till noon. From then on one would keep watch on the road and the store. The posse from the Wood River country should show up at the store some time shortly after noon. It wasn't likely that the pursuing posse could find their trail up that rocky dry wash, but they were averse to taking any reckless chances. They pulled off their boots and stretched their blankets on the mat of needles beneath a big pine tree.

Hawke woke with the sun beating into his face.

He rose, startled, and leaned over to waken Towers. "Come out of it," he said sharply. "It's after one o'clock. Round up the horses while I take a look at the road."

He jerked on his boots and hurried to the ridge west of the park. From the ridge one obtained an unobstructed view of the road leading from the store at the Crossing, and of a wide section of the barren and blackened lava beds. Into that region of fantastic shapes, for several miles, twisted a green delta in the ocean of black Lost River, swallowed finally by crevices and chasms of unknown depth. Hawke's eyes focussed on the sagebrush bottom east of the store. Eight men were riding across it, evidently the posse looking for the tracks of the fugitives' horses. The man-hunters had already advanced until they had reached a position within a mile of Travis and Towers, while those two were sleeping. Hawke hastened back with the unwelcome news.

They saddled their horses and packed their meager camp outfit, then both went to the ridge to look again at the posse. That determined band of men were approaching the dry wash. Should they find the faint tell-tale tracks, Travis and Towers would be forced into a dangerous position, cut off from the road to the east and from the west, forced to flee into the steep and rugged mountain range to the north. To the south there was no way of escape save over the lava beds on foot. But the man-hunters crossed the wash without pausing or turning.

And still the fugitives were undecided, whether they should try to escape over the range into northern Idaho or Montana, or wait till night and attempt to slip through the posse. Hawke had had enough of the north, he much preferred going on to Wyoming and Utah. The man-hunters would soon learn that the two had not kept on to the east, and it was not likely that the band would return to the Crossing to endeavor to pick up the trail there again. It was far more likely that they would go on to the next ranch and set a guard out for the fugitives, knowing well that the two would not dare to turn back and that they couldn't go south. Acting on that supposition, the fugitives decided to circle the ranch—which was the last one to the east for something like a hundred miles —and continue their course through the steep hills.

They were several miles from the ranch when night overtook them. Before leaving the foothills for the open plains to the right, they paused to let the horses feed. They themselves went without food, they were too near the enemy to risk a shot at game or a fire, and their cooked food was gone. When finally they reached the plains, they kept as far to the right of the road as the terrain permitted. As they approached a clump of brush two men sprang from a hiding place and leveled cocked six-shooters upon them. The night was fair and bright, the men plainly to be seen.

"Up, hombres. Stick 'em up—" one of them snapped.

But Hawke's hand darted to his belt. He shot the man's weapon from his hand, leaned low over the pommel of his saddle, sent a second warning shot at the other manhunter, and drove in his spurs. Towers followed him, his gun also belching flame into the darkness. The two dashed for the southeast, the man-hunters firing after them and shouting frantically for the other members of the posse. Evidently the band had placed a guard across the bottom between the lava beds and the hills.

As the fugitives raced on, they exchanged questions and opinions. The ground was sandy and would leave a trail regardless of the direction they took. There was only one safe place as an objective, Towers asserted, the Hole-in-the-Wall country. It lay to the northeast, beyond the Tetons. They did not dare to go south to Eagle Rock, Blackfoot, or any of the railroad towns. Their one chance was to outride the man-hunters. They were headed across the Snake River Desert, where it was unmercifully hot in the daytime and where there was no water for fifty miles. But the ground was hard and level, and the going was good, and they put the miles behind them. They stopped only once, to let the horses rest, but continued to press ahead until dawn. Swift desert dawn.

Across the sage-dotted desert, seemingly not more than thirty miles away in the clear air, white-capped and needle-pointed, rose the Three Tetons. Towers explained that Jackson's Hole was at the foot of Grand Teton. They would be safe once they arrived at that place. Hawke nodded, and turned his gaze from the peaks to the level region at the left.

"What's the lake this side of that peak?"

Towers' lean face lighted. "Mud Lake. Damned if I hadn't forgotten all about it. Plenty of grass for the horses there, but the mosquitoes are hell. But we can stop there till we cook the rest of our grub and eat. Then we'll fog for Market Lake."

The horses increased their plodding pace willingly, probably having sighted or smelled the water. Before Travis and Towers had reached the lake, their attention was attracted to some object, lying there on the plain between them and the lake's edge. At first, they thought it was a house, then a tent, but as they drew nearer it revealed itself to be a covered wagon. The two fugitives promptly rode up to it.

Beyond the dingy covered wagon a knobby-jointed, sway-backed horse was grazing on the scattered clumps of grass amongst the sage. Beyond it lay a dead horse. An emaciated man, with stooped shoulders and a weary face, was gathering sage-brush with which to replenish the campfire. A woman, fully as emaciated as he, was bending over the fire. She straightened, and both she and the man turned in wide-eyed surprise to gaze at the advancing riders.

"Good morning, folks," Hawke greeted them, drawing his horse to a halt. "How are the chances for something to eat at the Mud Lake Hotel?"

The thin man grinned dryly. "Pretty good, if you can be satisfied with what we've got." He turned to the woman. "Slice a little more bacon, Liz, and drap another handful of coffee into the pot. And fry that there sage hen we was aimin' to bile for dinner."

The woman nodded, smiling hospitably at the two riders.

Travis and Towers moved to some little distance from the camp to unsaddle their horses. Evidently this outfit camped here was as utterly a poverty-stricken outfit as Hawke had ever seen. He thought of the one-room cabin in Kansas. He had noted at least three or four children in the wagon, and he told himself the whole outfit hadn't enough clothes to wad a shotgun or grub to last a week. He never forgot the bitter poverty of his early childhood. Even to this day, nothing touches him quite so quickly, quite so poignantly arouses his sympathy, as sordid want and poverty. The deplorable state of the outfit occupied his mind as he and Towers left their hobbled mounts and returned to the fire, after refreshing themselves with a drink and washing in the lake.

The children were all out of the wagon now, emaciated and malnurtured like their parents, and were dressed and ready for their breakfast. Joe's warning about the mosquitoes was not exaggerated. As the eight people sat on their heels around the ragged old checkered tablecloth the woman had spread on the ground, they were forced to fight the pests continually. Hawke, interested, made an attempt to draw the man out, to learn something of him. It was not difficult. Misery may love company, as some saw-maker has asserted, but it loves far more to pour forth its woes into some sympathetic and listening ear. The man—his wife called him Ed—nodded his head vigorously when Hawke said it had been a dry season.

"It sure has. Me and Liz been tryin' to ranch down there in northern Utah. Couldn't make a go of it, account of sickness and lack of irrigatin' water. So I pulled for the north, intendin' to hit for the Wood River country. But old Nellie died on me shortly arter we got here. Reckon she foundered, or else jest played out. Put me in a bad hole. Ain't got the money to buy another hoss, nor no grub neither. I was thinkin', arter you fellas rid up, maybe I could git you to help me back to the railroad. I might git me a job on the section thar."

"I fancy we can help you out, Ed," Hawke replied. "Why don't you go on to the north? Plenty of good feed and water up that way, and plenty of open land, if that's what you're looking for. You can hitch my cayuse with yours and roll for the north."

Ed gazed wide-eyed in surprise and pleasure at the offer, mumbling that that would suit him fine. Towers stared at Travis with a puzzled scowl. What in hell was Hawke up to anyway? Hawke deliberately avoided his eyes, and rose with the others as Ed suggested it might be wise to get away from the mosquito-infested place. Puzzled, not knowing what to expect, Towers got his outfit and horse ready while Hawke helped Ed prepare the wagon for the continuance of his journey. Still silent and wondering, Joe rode in the lead till they reached the wagon road which paralleled the railroad running north and south. There Hawke called a halt and sprang from his seat beside Ed to the ground. He waved his hand at the road leading to the north.

"There's your road, Ed—and here's where I take another. So long, and good luck."

"But how about your hoss?" Ed eyed Hawke in amazement. "You aim to let me drive him all the way?"

Hawke shrugged. "Drive him anywhere you please. He's yours. And I'll throw in saddle, bridle, chaps and spurs. Won't need them where I'm going."

He stood smiling after the wagon as it rumbled off to the north, and Towers at last burst into angry speech.

"Now, ain't that a sweet trick? Settin' yourself afoot! You must be crazy with the heat! Any time you catch me hoofin' it when I got a posse on my trail, you can stick me in the bughouse."

"Well, what else could I do?" Hawke countered mildly. "Couldn't ride off and leave that poor devil and his woman and kids to starve there, could I?"

Towers snorted. "No use arguing, it's done. What next?"

"Oh, I may beat it for a way on the railroad. You still headed for Jackson's Hole?"

"I am. It's me for the wild bunch. Sorry you went and done that."

Hawke laughed. "Don't waste time being sorry about me. Beat it. I'll see you again, in hell—or Arizona."

So Joe Towers rode on, and Hawke Travis turned his steps toward the railroad. He was safer now from detection without the horse and rigging. No one but the Wood River officer had seen him with Towers. But since his act had forced separation upon them, the wisest thing he could do was to make himself appear as little like a cowboy as possible. Progress was awkward, in high-heeled boots, and as he went hobbling down the ties he decided to knock off the heels. His white Stetson was too conspicuous. He would trade that to the first hobo he met on the way to Blackfoot. He was saved the mutilation of his boots. He came to a section house, where he managed to steal a ride on a freight train which carried him into Blackfoot. He arrived in that town after dark, and would have aided his disguise by a clean shave could he have done so. The barber shops were all closed. He dined at a restaurant, and went into a general store to purchase a box of cartridges for his Colt.

The store was lighted by several kerosene lamps suspended from the ceiling. He paused at the open door to scrutinize the men within. There was nothing about the occupants of the room to rouse his suspicions. A half dozen Indians were strung along the counter, and perhaps as many white men were seated about the big stove near the center of the room. One lone customer was leaning on the cigar case which was situated within some twelve feet of the door and to the right of it. His complexion, garb and bearing indicated that he was a cattleman, but before Hawke had taken a second step toward the counter where he might purchase tobacco, he saw the "customer" straighten and eye him sharply.

He noted too the bulge under the lower part of the man's calf-skin vest. With a comprehensive glance at Hawke, the man started toward the door. But Hawke whirled in his tracks, whipped out his Colt and covered the man before he could shut him off from the door. At a command from Hawke, the officer raised both hands. Hawke stepped behind him and removed the Colt from the waistband of his trousers.

"Now back toward the door!" Hawke commanded, himself backing in that direction and covering the officer from behind. As he stepped across the threshold, one of the men in the transfixed group about the stove leaped up and came dashing toward him, reaching for his own weapon.

Hawke stopped him by sending a bullet through the crown of his hat. Then, wheeling, he dashed down the street, out a side street and into the brush and timber along the southern bank of the Snake River. Behind, he heard the excited yells of the citizens and the officer pursuing him, but it worried him little. They wouldn't continue that pursuit for any length of time. He was putting too much distance between himself and them. He slackened his pace presently to a swift walk, intending to keep straight on. But there were Indian teepees pitched in the river bottom, and to avoid them he was forced to swing to the right and again take his way into the sage-covered desert.

His situation was not too felicitous. He had only one round of shells, and the hunters were hard on his trail. He had set himself afoot to aid a poverty-ridden family, and, much as he hated to walk, walk he must, and stay away from towns and the railroad. He walked for most of the night.

In the early morning he came upon several milk cows in a pasture. He picked up an old empty tomato can that some cowpuncher had thrown away, filched a breakfast of warm milk from one of the cows, found a hiding place in thick brush and slept for several hours. After noon he proceeded toward the southeast. He had eluded his pursuers, but he was dog tired and ravenously hungry. As evening drew near he decided to risk a visit to the next ranch house he saw. It was dusk when he came to a log building, and was greeted by the barking of a shepherd dog. The dog's shrill clamor aroused someone within the house, and the door swung open before Hawke could reach it. A big heavy-chested man appeared in the doorway.

"What do you want?" he demanded, with nothing hospitable in his tone or face.

"Something to eat and a place to sleep for the night," Hawke answered, instant dislike for the man tensing him. "I can pay for the accommodation," he added curtly.

"We don't feed hoboes," the farmer snapped. Then he hesitated, as though an after thought had struck him. "Unless you happen to be a Latter-Day Saint?"

"A Latter-Day Saint?" Hawke grinned, coolly surveying the thick-chested man, who was dressed roughly in brogans, overalls and denim shirt. "So you're a Saint?" Hawke shook his head, as though he were viewing some rare and weird specimen of the animal kingdom. "No, glad to say, I'm not a Saint—Latter Day or otherwise." And he turned on his heel and walked away.

He told himself with a chuckle, "Well, we live and learn," and traveled briskly onward until there came into view the light from another ranch house some distance up the valley. At this place he met with a far different reception. He was invited into the house by its owner, a Mr. Todd, who received him cordially.

"Come right in. Of course you can have supper and a place to sleep, we never turn anyone away. Fortunately for you, we're a little late this evening. My name's Todd, Mister—?" He ended the sentence with a meaning upward inflection that hinted his desire to learn Hawke's name.

"Travis is the name," Hawke supplied quickly, as he removed his dusty Stetson and stepped inside the door Todd had swung open. "Commonly called Hawke."

Todd smiled. He was very tall, as dark as Hawke himself, and wore a heavy black beard. He made Hawke very thoroughly at home, and assured him that his daughter Ellen would have supper ready immediately. At the table Hawke met the others of the household, the slim, hardy daughter, Ellen, and Todd's hired man, Newton Lewis. Lewis was a likable, sandy-haired and freckled-faced youth of twenty-four. Todd was openly loquacious and sociable. Before the meal was over Hawke had learned that both the men and the girl were people he could like and respect. Todd was, in his own words, "strickly up against it," at that time. In that day and era such a condition was common among the settlers of the new country. Todd's worst stringency was lack of help. He needed more men to aid in putting up his hay.

Hawke thought quickly. The ranch was isolated. To hole up there for a month or so, quietly aiding in putting up that hay, would be good business for him. It might be a very smooth way of eluding the officers on his trail. He promptly offered his services, and they were as promptly accepted. He contemplated a quiet month in hiding! Quiet! If he could have looked ahead, he might not so readily have made that offer to Todd. So far as this particular gunman's blazing days were concerned, their mild beginning lay behind, and their multiplied activities loomed dead ahead.

III

Before that first evening was over, other aspects of Todd's situation came to light. The rancher frankly admitted that he would be extremely grateful for Hawke's aid in the haying, but that he had no money with which to pay wages, and had no prospect of getting any until after he had shipped some of the hay.

"You'll be lucky if you have any to ship," Newton Lewis hinted darkly.

To Hawke's raised brows of inquiry, Todd explained. The last winter's supply of hay had been burned, by some lawless fellows Todd called "the Rule outfit." The same outfit had been rustling his stock, to such an extent that Todd's finances and living facilities were badly impoverished. To Hawke's question as to where the Rule outfit hung out, Todd explained that Ephiram Rule owned the ranch at the lower end of the valley.

"You mean the Saint?" Hawke inquired, with a sudden broad grin.

"A Saint? Don't make me laugh," Todd snorted. "If Eph Rule's a Saint, then I'm a fit candidate for a harp and halo right now. But he isn't a fair sample of the Mormons, Hawke. Don't judge the Mormons by him. I'm certain he drove off my stock, but I can't prove it. If I dared accuse him, I wouldn't put it past him to burn my house and stable and kill my work horses. Anything to get me out of here. He wants the whole valley."

It didn't occur to Hawke that he was stepping into any particularly dangerous situation. Todd's story was an old one, in the Old West. Rustlers infested the country, they went to daring lengths and escaped penal reprisal in an astounding number of cases. The law had not too many agents then, and those it did have couldn't be every-where at once. "Judge Colt" certainly did admin-istrate his own law largely, in many cases wisely, and very frequently met with no opposition or censure from the Federal and County authorities. He had his day. Eph Rule was making the most of it, as numerous ones of his kind did.

That night Newton showed Hawke to his room, and Hawke frowned at the clean sheets, thinking of his sweaty and dust-begrimed body. He said as much, and Newton offered to bring in a tub of warm water. Hawke accepted the offer with alacrity and began to undress. Newton delivered the tub full of water, and a clean suit of his own underwear. Hawke looked him rather levelly in the eye.

"I've been traveling for several days without let-up or rest," he said significantly.

Newton's eyes twinkled. "On the dodge, eh? Do you know, I rather thought so. But that makes no difference so far as I'm concerned, and it won't make any difference with Todd. Your business is your own. If you're willing to help us get in that hay, you're welcome to this ranch as a place of— let's say retirement."

Hawke laughed. "Many thanks. I don't usually deceive anyone who's kind enough to aid me when I'm—ah—traveling for my health. Before you go, would you mind giving me a concise summary of Todd's situation, this Rule outfit, and so on? I'm not sure I see through the whole thing yet."

Newton sat down on the edge of the bed, while Hawke stepped into the tubful of warm water, and proceeded with the explanation Hawke had requested.

"It's a worse situation than Todd let on to you. Eph Rule has an eye on Ellen, which is part of his reason for persecuting Todd. He's insane enough to think that he can force Todd to favor his courting Ellen if he bears down hard enough, and that Ellen would favor him if her father desired it. Eph and Sam Rule are in hunk with the Red Desert Gang. They ran off Todd's stock, and Eph and Sam sold them to butchers and ranchers in the valley around Bear Lake. The Red Desert Gang rustles stock along the Oregon Trail and over in Wyoming, and as 'honest ranchers' Eph and Sam dispose of the stock. Sam's homestead lays across the mouth of the gulch leading up to the only good pass over the range to the southwest. He controls the pass and can drive stock over it any time after the snow goes off, without being bothered by anyone.

"You might ask what's the matter with the sheriff of Bannock County and the Wyoming officers. They haven't much chance. Sheriff Duncan's been after the gang a time or two, but he's never been able to catch them on this side of the line. Their hangout's in Wyoming, supposed to be in the Salt River Range. That's devilish wild country, and a long way from the county seat. So they have their own way. They can keep on having it for all of me. I wouldn't go over there after them on a bet. That Butch McKelvey's a two-gun man, it's claimed, and has got notches on both guns."

Hawke smiled dryly. "What of it? He isn't the only gunman in the country."

Newton eyed him intently for a moment, then shifted his gaze to the long-barreled Colt Hawke had taken from his waistband and hung on a nail driven into a log near the head of the bed. "Yeh? Well, I kind of thought that too, Hawke. But, me, I'm not looking for any row. I'd rather pull out and lose all we've got here than go up against that outfit."

Hawke changed the subject. He remarked that he would feel much better for a clean shave, and Newton went out to fetch a razor. Under what Newton had said, Hawke divined other things he did not say. Newton himself had an interest in the ranch, and was far more than mere hired man and neighboring homesteader. He had an interest in the girl, too, which doubled his resentment against Ephiram Rule for daring to aspire to the girl. Hawke began to sense faintly that things around here might grow interesting before he moved on.

After breakfast the next morning, he accompanied Newton to a patch of alfalfa Newt had planted at the lower end of his homestead, which adjoined the south line of Todd's holdings. The line ran between Newton's cabin and Todd's ranch house. Newton's errand was to change the water in the irrigation ditch. He called Hawke's attention to the possibilities of the place. There was excellent soil, quantities of wood and pure mountain water. Also, back in the hills, there was enough excellent range to run at least five thousand head of stock.

"It's the kind of place a fellow could make a big stake out of," Newton declared vehemently, "if he didn't have to fight that damned Rule outfit tooth and nail every foot of the way. It's a wonder they didn't locate this ground too when they filed on the lower end of the valley. I believe the only reason they didn't was that they used up all their rights down there, and couldn't get any friends of theirs to file for them. They did claim these quarters, and they might have bluffed us out if Todd hadn't gone to the land office and looked at the records."

"I believe you have a visitor approaching,

Newt," Hawke cut in, with a gesture toward the valley.

Newton whirled and stared at the horseman coming toward them. "Eph Rule. That's his roan. Damn him! I wish I'd brought my Winchester. He threatened to beat my head off the next time he caught me using water out of Willow Creek. The outfit claims all of it. I hate to run from him, but I hate worse to get beaten up by him. He's thirty pounds heavier, and strong as a bull."

Hawke glanced toward the rider, less than a quarter mile away. "Use your shovel on him," he drawled. "If that fails—" He flipped up the bottom of his vest and drew his Colt with such bewildering speed that Newton stared as if he were wondering from what source it had come. He extended the gun toward Newton. "Remember what a certain gunman had engraved on the butt of his Colt?

> 'Fear not the wrath of any man
>   who walks beneath the skies,
> Though he be great, and you be small;
>   for I will equalize.'

Take old Betsy. She'll make you the equal of Eph Rule or any other man."

Newton shook his head quickly. "I'm no gunman. He'd probably take it away from me and bend it over my head if I drew it on him. Better put it up before he sees it."

Hawke nodded, and the weapon disappeared as quickly as it had appeared. In his blue serge vest and shirt sleeves, Hawke looked deceptively harmless. That was characteristic of him. When he looked most harmless, seemed most suave and inert, he was in reality most deadly and on the alert, ready to strike. He turned his attention to Rule. The big man had dismounted at the Todd corral, two hundred yards below the alfalfa field, and was now striding toward Travis and Lewis, his big spurs jingling, his chaps scuffling between his legs. He was patently in a very bad humor, for his face was set in a scowl as he approached. He glanced at Hawke, who had thrust into the ground the shovel he had brought and was leaning on the handle. But Rule's first remark was directed at Lewis.

"Didn't I tell you to leave this water alone?"

"Sure," Lewis agreed curtly. "And didn't I tell you to go to hell? This water is mine according to the laws of this State. It makes no difference if you did file on the creek first, you can't hold more of the water than you need for irrigation."

"Can't, eh?" Rule's scowl grew belligerent. "We'll see about that. Have you forgot what I promised you if I caught you taking this water again?"

"Hop right to it." Lewis's face paled slightly, but he gripped the handle of his shovel in a threat that needed no words.

Rule read the threat instantly, and his hand darted down to the six-shooter in his holster. "Drop that shovel! Make a move and I'll drill you. Drop it!" he commanded, half drawing the gun. His gaze flashed to Hawke. "That goes for you, too."

Lewis ignored the order, and gripped the shovel determinedly, holding it poised and ready to strike. Rule jerked out his gun. But Hawke had him beaten with nice calculation. The forty-four was out of its waistband habitation and in Hawke's hand, roaring, before Eph's draw was completed. The bullet it spat thudded into the wood of the stock of the gun Eph held. He dropped it very promptly. The middle finger of his right hand dangled from a stump from which the blood spurted. The change in his manner was ludicrous. From blusterer he turned to frightened suer for peace.

"Don't shoot again!" he said sharply. "For God's sake don't shoot again. I'll bleed to death!"

Hawke laughed with a dry contempt in his face. He calmly disposed of his smoking gun, drew from his pocket a clean bandana Lewis had lent him and proceeded to bandage the finger. Todd came running from his own field, having seen Rule approach and having heard the shot. By the time he arrived, Hawke had stopped all flowing of the blood by twisting a tourniquet around the stump of the finger. He assisted Rule to his horse and into the saddle, with the other following at his heels. As Rule picked up the reins in his left hand, he recovered some of his arrogance.

"I'll get you for that," he snarled at Hawke. "And don't think I won't. But first I'm going to see what Bishop Sommers has to say about a dangerous gunman being in his precinct. He'll bind you over for assault with a deadly weapon, and you'll get about ten year in Boise pen for what you've done to me."

Some of Hawke's suavity vanished in impatience. "Don't be an utter fool, Rule. Just dare to make a case of this and bring it to court! You'll be the one who'll go over the road. Newt saw you pull your gun, and threaten to shoot both of us, so you'd better forget it. And you'd better beat it, and consider yourself lucky to get off so easy."

"Reckon he's right," Todd put in. "I saw the whole performance, and would testify that Mr. Travis would have been justified had he shot you down in your tracks."

"Why, you—you was away over there in your own field!" Rule sputtered.

"Not at all," Todd denied blandly. "I was standing right there and saw the whole business. Wasn't I, Newt?"

"Sure was," Newt agreed laconically.

"Most certainly you were, Mr. Todd," Hawke affirmed, and turned to Rule. He repeated, inelegantly but very forcefully, "Beat it!"

Rule sank his spurs into his big roan and shook his bandaged right hand. "Damn your souls to hell!" he shouted furiously. "I'll be back and wipe out the whole bunch of you!"

Hawke calmly turned his back as Rule rode away, and asked in a lowered tone: "What has this Bishop Sommers to do with the law in this neck of the woods, Mr. Todd? Justice of the Peace?"

Todd nodded, but Lewis hastened to explain. " 'Old Whiskers,' as they call him, is the big noise in this end of the country. He rules the Saints, and favors them when it comes to a showdown between the Saints and a Gentile. As a matter of fact, I guess you had better duck if he sends a constable after you. You wouldn't have no more chance than a snowball in hell if they dragged you into that court."

"Yes?" Hawke's black eyes sparked. "Well, there are times when I run, and there are times when I do not. This is one of the times I do not. It seems as if I was born to trouble, as the sparks fly upward. The worst of it is that I'm always getting somebody else into a mess—and I hate a fight as the devil hates holy water." Oddly enough, that was the truth. Perhaps, the very fact that he did dislike "ructions," (his term), and his resentment when he seemed continually to be running into them, influenced his very fury of action whenever a fight was precipitated upon him. I don't mean to say that he actively avoided a gun fight; on the contrary he often went after one with whole-souled ardor; but by some twist of circumstances he was always thrust into a situation which made the fight imperative or advisable—from his angle at least—before he went after it. Which may seem involved and contradictory, but is not if you'll figure it out for yourself.

The three men stood by the corral, after Rule had disappeared, talking over the situation. Todd raised the subject of another possibility.

"That's hardly what he'll do, though, to my way of thinking, Travis. Have you arrested, I mean. He'll be back as he threatened, but he'll bring the Red Desert Gang with him, intending to wipe us out and be done with it. He realizes how much protection he has."

"In other words, I seem to have precipitated a showdown," Hawke suggested mildly. "Is that it?"

"Well, I fancy you have started something," Todd admitted with some reluctance. "I can't say that I'm sorry. Might as well know exactly where we stand and have it over. The continual striving against that outfit wears a man out. If the Rules *are* in with Butch McKelvey and his gang, there'll be some scrap. I think I'll send Ellen to her aunt in Pocatello tomorrow. They won't waste much time about acting, that gang. We'd better go over to the house, oil up the rifles and see how we're fixed for ammunition."

"Let 'em act," Hawke retorted. "I never started anything I couldn't finish."

Ellen, worried and apprehensive, met the men as they entered the house. The living room faced the corral and stables, and she had seen enough to give her some idea of what had happened. Her father told her he was sending her to her aunt the next day. Her eyes flared.

"I'm not going a step. I can shoot and I can ride, and you're going to need everybody that can handle a gun. I have enough sense to keep under cover and not expose myself to danger. Am I not right, Mr. Travis?"

"Well, it is sometimes safer to fight than run," Hawke admitted. "You may not have time to get away. From what your father says they might be on us tonight. Unless it takes Rule a day or two to get his gang together. But, when they do show up, we want to remember that if you have to fight it's safer to beat the other fellow to it."

"And what do you mean by that?" Todd demanded.

Hawke shook his head, smiling. "That would be telling. Wait and see. But I know a thing or two about fighting."

"With guns?" Newton drawled, and Hawke laughed aloud.

"That's for me to know and you to find out."

Ellen busied herself with the housework, while the three men cleaned and oiled two Winchesters,

Newton's long-barreled Smith and Wesson revolver and Hawke's forty-four. Todd had two boxes of forty-four shells, so Hawke's ammunition was supplied. They were ready in short time for any raiders. Yet, two monotonous weeks went by and all they did was make hay. Nevertheless, Hawke and Newton Lewis went armed to the hay field every day. Rule's inaction did not deceive any of them. To prevent anyone's setting fire to the growing stacks of hay, Travis dug a hole in the top of one of the huge stacks, and passed the nights there, armed with his six-shooter and a ten-gauge shotgun.

Ellen had set herself the task of riding out on her pony and keeping a lookout to prevent if possible their being taken by surprise. But Todd commanded her to stay safely close, and she had seen nothing to indicate vengeful movement on the part of the Rules. So the two weeks went by.

Hawke was nervous and high strung. Some peculiar intuition seemed on the alert in his mind at all times, to warn him when danger impended. This particular night he had gone to sleep in the haystack. It was somewhere around eleven o'clock when he wakened suddenly, as though startled by a bell that had rung a warning. Mechanically, he sat up, blinked the sleep from his eyes, gazing about. As mechanically, he snatched up the shotgun. Several dim figures were coming up the valley, figures which, nearing and spreading, revealed themselves as horsemen, riding straight toward the Todd ranch house. Hawke cocked both hammers of the shotgun, and waited, motionless, to see what the men intended. Two of them, nearest the center of the advancing line, came within fifty yards of him, and one of them spoke, his words carrying clearly to the alert gunman in the haystack.

"You aim to round up the bunch of 'em before you set fire to the outfit, Butch?"

A scornful snort came from the man addressed. "Think I'm such a damn fool as to make a light for 'em to pot us before we can get within a hundred yards of them? Of course we'll take 'em into camp first. But no killin'. I can't afford to have all the sheriffs and deputies in the State trailin' me. Besides, killin' ain't necessary. We can get 'em easy enough. What you do to that jasper that shot yuh is nothin' to me. But do it after we hit the trail for the hangout. Move along, now."

The other one made some sort of affirmative answer and they started to dismount. Hawke promptly raised the shotgun and discharged both barrels squarely at them. The detonation of the heavy charges split the silence of the night with a resounding boom. It was followed by the squealing and snorting of the horses, by surprised and furious yells from the men. The two mounts of the men at whom Hawke had fired reared and went galloping away, sending their half-dismounted riders sprawling. A shot rang out from the vicinity of Lewis's cabin, and a spurt of flame flashed from one of the windows in the ranch house. Hawke broke the shotgun and shoved fresh shells into the breech. The flash of shots in several directions about the ranch house gave evidence that the Rule outfit had recovered from its surprise and was returning the fire.

Hawke slid to the ground on the side of the stack opposite the corral and slipped behind the baler. The baler stood outside the stackyard, and from behind it Hawke could command both house and stable. It was too dark for him to locate the raiders except by the flashes of their guns. But a man with a keen eye can do some nice calculating by the lurid flash a gun makes in the night. At those flashes he opened up a rapid-fire one-man war, emptying first the shotgun and then the Colt, reloading them and emptying them again. He had no way of knowing whether or not he was doing any real damage; he could be guided only by the frequent curses and yells that responded to his fire. They might be yells or curses of pain. He never did know, for a certainty, what toll his one-man war demanded of the enemy.

Manifestly he, as he says, did succeed in "putting the fear of God into 'em," for they departed within a very few minutes. Hawke's reception had been altogether too hot for them. Their firing ceased. A few seconds later Hawke heard the drumming of hooves on the turf of the meadow below the ranch buildings. Temporarily at least, the Rule outfit was routed. Hawke went on the run to the house, calling to Todd:

"Hello the house! The war's over. Don't take a crack at me!"

Newton came running from his cabin to join them in the house, was right behind Hawke. He heard Todd say as he came in the door:

"Is it over, or have you mis-stated the situation?"

Hawke grinned, but the grin was wry and without mirth. His hot temper was up, and believe you me, when Hawke's temper is up there's something doing! He looked Todd straight in the eye, and answered meaningly: "Well, if I was running the show, I'd go after that gang, hot-foot, and without losing any time. They'll be back, with augmented numbers. Remember, if you have to fight, beat the other fellow to it. I'd go after 'em so hot and heavy they'd never know what hit 'em!"

"All right, go after 'em," Todd returned mildly. "I'll go with you."

Newton cried out in approval. "Let's clean our artillery and hit the trail."

"Not so fast," Hawke cut in. "See here, Mr. Todd. This is going to be some scrap. You're an older man. You'd better stay here and look after the ranch and Miss Ellen."

"I'm going with you and Newt," Ellen interrupted, "I'm not going to stay here."

"Oh, yes you are," Hawke contradicted curtly. "Those hombres will shoot to kill, and they won't at all care who they're killing. You'll stay here with your father, and that's that." He ignored the girl's resentful, angry eyes and turned to Todd. "You admit you're no gunman, Mr. Todd. Well—I am. Leave this to Newt and me."

"I've nothing to say—apparently," Todd returned, smiling humorously. "I guess you're running the show all right. Go to it."

Hawke proceeded without loss of time. He and Lewis hurried out to the pasture to secure mounts. They found the riding stock and work horses unmolested. The rustlers had been driven off in too great a hurry to have time to take any of the horses with them. Some one of the band of raiders had let down the bars. Hawke and Lewis herded the horses into the corral, saddled two of them and went riding down the valley, leaving Todd at the corral, armed with the shotgun. Lewis carried one of the Winchesters, they had left the other in the house with the girl. Hawke was armed only with his Colt. When they reached a position within a quarter-mile of the Rule place, Hawke called a halt.

"What do you make of that light, Newt? Up there in the hills northeast of the house. Anyone live up there?"

"No," said a voice behind him. "Not a soul."

Hawke whirled in the saddle, an impatient

curse on his lips. It was Ellen Todd. "What are you doing here?" he demanded.

"Following you," she retorted. "I said I was coming."

Hawke cursed soulfully, and turned abruptly to Lewis. "Far be it from me to try to argue with a woman. What's that light doing up there? Campfire?"

"Likely," Newton replied. "It's rough country over there. Fit for nothing but stock. Might be the Red Desert Gang."

Hawke stared at the light. It was caused by the reflection of a hidden fire, and it glowed somberly on a clump of conifers, flaring and dying down alternately as if the fire were being fed by resinous limbs. "You know, we didn't see anything of the cattle when we went to get the horses. How do we know there weren't more of that gang, and that the others were busy driving off the stock while Eph and his outfit engaged our attention at the house? I think we'll ride up there and see what we find."

The three of them swung round in back of the Rule place and rode toward the intermittent glow. Little time was needed to cover the distance. In a grove of scrubby pine Travis again called a halt and dismounted. "Come along, Newt. We'll take it afoot from here. Miss Ellen, you stay with the horses while we see who has that fire there."

"I'm going with you," the girl insisted stubbornly.

"You're staying right here," Hawke corrected her. "Think I want those horses run off and us left afoot? You've got yourself a job. You would come, so do your share. Watch the horses."

The girl made no answer, but she dismounted and stood quietly by the animals and Hawke and Lewis started off up the gulch leading away from them.

The two men presently rounded a bend in the gulch and came within sight of a small fire. They paused and looked intently ahead of them. Hawke lighted a match, screening it with his hand, and examined the floor of the gulch. Many tracks testified to the fact that several head of cattle and a few horses recently had gone up the gulch. Hawke straightened and remained motionless for a moment, thinking it over. Then he turned to Lewis. "I've a plan. We'll split here. I'll go up the left-hand side of the gulch, you go up the right. We'll work our way above their camp till we reach the stock, and stampede the cattle down the gulch. Miss Ellen and the horses are well out of the way. And if we send several head of frightened cattle stampeding through those hombres' camp I reckon they'll move. And we'll move after 'em."

"Shoot to kill?" Lewis inquired grimly.

"Not unless we have to. But I aim to fix them so they won't do any more rustling for a while."

Travis was playing a desperate game, and he realized it fully. But when he took the offensive,

58

he took it with a will. Keeping to the left-hand hillside, he reached a position opposite the campfire, and grinned to himself. The camp was in the bottom of the gulch, would be squarely in the path of the stampeding cattle should the animals be started down the gully. About the fire were seven as villainous looking men as he had ever seen in or out of jail. They were garbed like cowboys, and lounged about the fire smoking and talking. Hawke went on, leaving them behind; continued on for a good quarter-mile before he came to that part of the gully in which the cattle had been left. They were distinctly visible, dark blotches in the gully bed. There must be a guard about somewhere, and Hawke waited quietly, till by some sign the man should betray his presence and his position.

He betrayed it by striking a match to light a cigaret. Promptly Hawke fired at him, and yelled at the top of his voice. From the opposite hillside, Lewis answered and fired a responding shot. The guard let out a veritable squeal. As he had raised the match to light his cigaret, taking no care to shield it since there was no wind, the glow had revealed his hand and face clearly for a moment. That moment had been quite enough for Hawke. With a ball through the palm of his hand and his gun-fanning ability sadly wrecked, the guard fled as fast as his feet could carry him toward the camp. Hawke and Lewis plunged down the hillside, toward each other, toward the gully bed and toward the cattle, yelling and firing their guns as they ran.

The cattle grunted and got to their feet. The grunts became frightened bawls. In a very few moments the herd was in panicky flight, accompanied by the drum of pounding hooves and the click of horns. Lewis and Travis followed the cattle. The animals got far ahead of them, and frightened yells and scattering shots rose from the camp below in the gully. Then all sound died away, and Travis and Lewis cautiously approached the camp. The rout had been complete.

The camp was in the utmost confusion. The fire had been scattered and was almost out. Three or four saddles, a half dozen blankets and tarpaulins, lay about; among them was scattered a litter of battered cooking utensils. One of the rustlers, wrapped in his blankets and evidently asleep when the herd charged upon the camp, still lay where he had been, battered to death by the hooves of the cattle.

"Well, we put the fear of God into them, all right," Hawke commented. "Now we'll hurry down and make certain that Miss Ellen is all right. If she stayed where we left her, she is in no danger."

But, as they learned later, the bull-headed and stubborn girl had again disobeyed orders. She had deliberately tried to follow them, and run squarely into the fleeing rustlers. When Travis and

Lewis reached the grove, there was no sign of the girl or the horses. Hawke's alert brain leaped to the probable solution of her disappearance. Lewis went wild, and blurted a dozen lurid threats. Hawke calmly seated himself with his back against a pine tree.

"Cool down, Newt, and sit down. I'm going to get my breath before we go on. They won't hurt the girl. They ran into her some way and took her and the horses along. They'll probably take her to Rule's place."

"I don't think they will," Lewis protested. "Old Sam is an elder in the church and a lot better than the rest of them. I don't think he knows the extent of the deviltry them boys are up to. No, they'll take her to the hangout of the Red Desert Gang. They'll probably hold her and make all kinds of silly threats, and try to force me and Todd to agree to get out and leave the valley to them. But we can't sit around here like this, Hawke. Of course they won't hurt her, but do you think it's going to be very pleasant for her holed up with that gang?"

Hawke rose. "Don't worry, Newt. They'll get no chance to subject her to any indignities. We've got to have horses first, so we'll beat it for the ranch and get going."

At ten o'clock the next morning, Hawke and Newton Lewis had reached a place on the watershed between the Salt River and Hamsfork of the Bear, an elevation which commanded a view of all the high and broken terrain between them and the Salt River Range thirty miles or more away to the northeast. To the north, dominating the low ranges and black buttes lying between, the three needle peaks of the Teton Range gleamed in the morning sun. They had with them now the very anxious father of the girl. At Hawke's insistence they had waited till daylight to trail the rustlers.

They were traveling light and making good time. The trail had led up another gulch and across the valley from the Rule place, where the gang had evidently gone to secure fresh mounts. The trail was fresh. Hawke judged they were not more than three hours behind their quarry, and perhaps a distance of ten miles was all the lead the rustlers had. The trail led upward continually till it reached the divide. As they paused to rest their panting horses, Lewis pointed to a low mountain almost directly east. Beyond it, in hazy distance, loomed a white peak that dominated the Wind River Range.

"The low one's Mount Wagner, the peak is Fremont Peak. The way this trail's been heading, I'd guess that them rustlers are holed up over there near the base of Wagner at the southern end of the Salt River Range. Think we can run 'em into their hole before night?"

"If we keep going," Hawke replied, and urged his horse ahead.

A short distance onward, they came to the ashes of a late campfire which had been built near a small stream bordered by quaking aspen and willow. Evidently the rustlers had stopped there for breakfast. Here too was evidence of the fact that the girl was with them, her boot-tracks in the ground about the ashes. Hawke and Todd decided to pause here for a meal, and to allow the horses a short rest. After eating, they went on, following the trail across comparatively open country until they were convinced that the gang was certainly traveling toward Mount Wagner. Then, acting upon Hawke's advice, they swung a half mile to the right and took a course parallel with the trail, to avoid the danger of being surprised by some lookout the Red Desert Gang might have left to cover their retreat.

Just before dusk, the three swung back to the trail, finding it still leading south and east toward the south end of the Salt River Range. This was now but five or six miles away. The ground was open and timber none too plentiful. But they saw no signs anywhere of a campfire. They continued onward for another three miles, until the country became so broken that traveling after night was rendered difficult and dangerous. They halted and camped in a gulch, eating cold food and not risking a fire. After they had eaten, and tethered their horses, they decided to investigate the region to the north and east. They climbed a ridge which commanded a view of most of the region they had covered during the day, and of the country to the north. But they saw no firelight to evidence the presence of the Red Desert outfit. They returned to their camp, and the question of food rose as a most important one to be considered.

They must have more food than the light supply they had brought, now almost exhausted. There was no telling how long this chase might string out. The next morning Newton shot a deer, and they risked building a fire. They cooked a good supply of venison, placed it in their empty flour sack, and put the sack in one of the saddlebags. They then returned to the rustlers' trail. It did not lead over the range. The hangout was within three miles of their own camp. In less than two hours they had discovered it.

It was situated in a thick grove of scrubby pine at the head of a wide valley sloping down to the country west of the range. The hillside in back of the camp rose at a steep angle, and was thickly covered with scrub cedar, stunted pines and some brush. Near a spring at the foot of the hill was a sod-roofed log cabin. Not far from the camp several horses were feeding, in charge of a lone guard. Some distance below, they made out the figure of another man, evidently posted as lookout to keep watch to the west. Manifestly, any attempt to assail the camp in the daytime would have been a very indiscreet move.

Travis and the other two men returned to their own camp, to wait for nightfall. At dusk they returned to the spot from which they had been watching the rustler camp. Several men were gathered about a fire built at one side of the clearing surrounding the cabin. A soiled tent had been erected a short way beyond them. Hawke gazed down at them sharply. There was no telling how many more might be in the cabin; not many, he thought. He counted eight by the fire. Those sitting by the fire could not see the door of the cabin from their position, he calculated. A small knot of scrubby pine stood between them and the cabin. Hawke nodded to himself, and turned to Lewis.

"Well, I guess we're ready to go. I'll hit for the cabin. You stay outside and stand off the others, in case I have to shoot."

"In case you have to shoot!" jeered Lewis. "What are you going in there for?"

"I fancy that's where they have Miss Ellen," Hawke answered. "But this time, if you have to shoot, shoot to kill. Both of you. I'm off."

Travis slipped down to the foot of the bluff and approached the back of the cabin. He paused for a moment, listening intently. There were more men within the cabin. He could hear the murmur of voices. He drew his Colt, walked around the cabin to the front door, kicked it open and coolly walked in.

The interior was lighted by a candle which had been thrust into the neck of an empty beer bottle. The bottle was placed on a rough plank table. Two men sat on opposite sides of the table, eating. One, squat and heavy, a man of forty years of age or more, sat at Hawke's left. He wore two guns, the six-shooters sagging the sides of his belt, their holsters tied down to his legs. He dropped knife and fork, sprang to his feet, kicked over his stool and reached for his guns as Hawke commanded him to put up his hands.

This man was Butch McKelvey, a rabid outlaw of many aliases and many crimes, a man much feared and with a reputation of ruthless killer. He paid no least heed to Hawke's command. In a split second granted him for thought, Hawke knew that he must kill or be killed. Butch McKelvey granted no quarter. Without an instant's hesitation, Hawke shot him through the head, then turned the smoking muzzle of his Colt on the other man. This one promptly threw up both hands. Ellen Todd was standing by the fireplace.

"Miss Ellen," Hawke said dryly. "If you can do what you're told for once, grab that fellow's gun and run for the back of the cabin. Newt's there. He'll show you the way to go."

This time Ellen Todd obeyed. Her fascinated eyes jerked from the dead body of McKelvey, she snatched from its holster the gun belonging to the other man, and dashed out the door. As she ran, Hawke heard Newt and Todd open fire on the others. At the sound of Hawke's shot the other outlaws had leaped up from the fire and started for the cabin. Todd and Newt had opened fire on them to protect and warn Hawke.

As Hawke had entered, he had stepped out of line with the door. The other outlaw still sat on his stool, hands upraised, his eyes on Hawke's smoking forty-four.

"Get out of here!" Hawke commanded.

The man sprang from his seat and darted to the door, and fell face down on the threshold, shot through many times. The advancing band had fired a volley on the cabin, and they killed their own man as he leaped for the door. Now the girl proved her assertion that she could shoot. She had reached Newt and her father, and made good use of the gun she had taken from the outlaw. Under the concerted fire the outlaws gave ground and made for cover. Hawke divined it by a short lull in the firing. A Henry rifle hung in a deer-horn rack on the wall, a belt full of shells by it. Hawke snatched down rifle and belt and flashed out the door. The rest of the gang fired at him, but he was an indistinct, darting figure and not a bullet touched him. He darted out of range into the timber behind the cabin. There he joined the other three, and, at his curt order, they made speedy departure toward their camp and their horses.

It is very true that a band of men is as rapacious and dangerous as its leader, and no more so. The deadly Butch McKelvey had fallen. The sting was taken out of the Red Desert Gang. What further depredations they may have committed Hawke never knew. It is likely they scattered. At all events, they never again molested Todd, and Ephiram Rule evidently learned a harsh lesson. His brother, young Sam Rule, had been the man who was battered to death by the stampeding steers. Eph turned quiet and let Todd severely alone, contenting himself by evidencing his resentment in a leering scowl when he chanced to meet the rancher. That knowledge came to Hawke later in a roundabout way. He, Hawke, with Lewis, Todd and the girl, returned from the raid to the Todd ranch in a speedy and unhindered journey. There the chapter of the Todds closes, so far as Hawke's life is concerned. Todd's haying was finished. The theft of the horses in the Boise fracas was probably forgotten. Hawke grew restless to move on.

Within a week he did move. In lieu of wages for his work in the hay field, Todd presented Hawke with a horse and rigging. And one fair morning, Hawke Travis, gunman and fugitive, having paused, and served, and fought, and killed, mounted and rode away.

IV

He continued his journey eastward along the old Oregon Trail. By now he was convinced that the Idaho authorities had ceased searching for him. For a week he traveled, and in that week nothing of moment transpired. Crossing the sage-brush flat lying between the Big Sandy and the Little Sandy, he saw ahead of him a man camped on the bank of the smaller stream. Feeling certain that there was little likelihood of the man's being an officer, he made no attempt to avoid being seen by the camper. He rode straight ahead to the ford, pausing to let his mount drink, and turned a scrutinizing gaze on the man and his fire, perhaps a hundred yards downstream. The man's back was toward him, but the tall, supple body seemed familiar.

Hawke turned his gaze to the horse nosing for bunchgrass amongst the sage. The animal was a large roan. It also looked familiar. It should, Hawke told himself, since it was doubtlessly the very horse that had galloped by his own mount when he had left Boise behind. He raised his voice in a hail:

"Hey, there, you old horse thief! Haven't they got you yet?"

The man at the fire straightened and whirled,

and his right hand made a half movement toward the butt of the Colt in his holster. Then he laughed delightedly. "Well, I'll be damned if I ever expected to see you again. I thought you'd be gone into the Wind River country or into Utah long ago. Come on down here and give an account of yourself."

Travis turned his mount toward the fire, and again he joined his fortunes with those of Joe Towers. He put his horse out to graze and over the meal they exchanged notes. Towers had intended to proceed to the Hole-in-the-Wall. But after separating from Hawke he had stopped with a nester near the Idaho and Wyoming line. He had aided the nester in doing his fall work. That finished he had traveled on, rather aimlessly, merely to be going, still with a half notion in his head to reach the Wind River country sooner or later.

"I've about decided to go to Lander," Towers finished the account of his doings. "Sound good to you?"

"It makes little difference which way I go," Hawke replied. "What do you intend doing over Lander way? Go back to punching cows?"

"I might. But the first chance I get I'm going to hop onto a good piece of land. A man don't need much to start him up in the cow business in this wooden country." Towers grinned impishly. "Nothing much but a lot of nerve and a running iron."

"Then you ought to make a success of it," Hawke returned. "You have the nerve, and it won't cost much for the running iron. All right, we'll go to Lander."

So easily do men make decisions. But—so easily are those decisions sometimes unexpectedly nullified by events. Hawke was awakened at dawn by the boom of a gun, and leaped up, fearful of seeing officers bearing down on him and his companion. He saw nothing but Joe Towers literally jumping up and down in excitement, and in his underclothes, a smoking Winchester in his hand.

"What the devil's coming off?" Hawke snapped, automatically reaching for his Colt. "Damn your hide, you woke me out of a sweet sleep. What's the big idea? Think this is the Fourth of July?"

"The big idea is venison for breakfast," Towers answered, scowling in chagrin. "I fired at a big buck. He was drinking in the stream. Hit him, too. He dropped to his knees and then went bouncing off upstream. Damn it anyhow, had to go and lose him."

Hawke grinned, laid his Colt down, and hurriedly donned his trousers and boots.

"You build a fire and grease the old frypan. I'll take the Winchester and get the buck."

He hurried off with the rifle, and Towers energetically set about dressing himself and building a fire. The buck's trail was very plain, and a sprinkling of blood along the way proved that the animal had been hit. But he still retained an astounding amount of vitality. Hawke trailed him swiftly but the deer managed to keep out of range. Hawke saw the animal several times, and continued after him determinedly. A man can travel a long way after game, with the continual thought in mind that he may catch up with his quarry at the next turn. Hawke traveled a little better than six miles before he finally gave it up in disgust, and concluded that the deer wasn't so badly wounded as he had thought.

The sun was high enough now to make itself felt, and he was overheated from the zest of the chase. He paused to take a drink at the stream, and looked about him. In his haste to get the deer he had neglected to snatch up his hat. He didn't like the sun on his head. With some twigs of willow and cedar, and two or three handfuls of long, tough grass, he wove a rough mat and put it on his head. To keep it there, he twisted a rope of grass and tied it on, then got to his feet and picked up his rifle.

"With apologies to my boyhood friend, Crusoe," he told himself with a grin. "All I need now is a parasol and a man Friday."

He started to leave the stream, and stopped short, whirling to glance at a ridge off to his right. He had heard the snort of a horse. Above the tops of the scrubby trees on the ridge he saw a feather of smoke rising. Doubtlessly someone was camped there. He might step over and beg a cup of coffee before returning to join Joe. It was a long walk back to camp, and the chase after the deer had made him hungry.

He climbed briskly to the top of the ridge, and found himself looking down into a clearing in the thick timber. Fifteen or more horses were grazing at the edge of the clearing, work horses. Two men were squatted by a dying campfire, smoking after their breakfast. Hawke scowled and decided to keep away from them. They were a tough-looking pair. Some of the horses showed harness galls. The men might belong to one of the bands of rustlers who had been known to be engaged in running off stock from ranches down toward Green River. Hawke started to back noiselessly from sight, before they should glance up and see him.

He stopped short, though, when he heard a rasping voice from behind him:

"Drop it and stick 'em up, you!"

He did not drop his rifle, but he whirled to find himself looking into the muzzle of a threatening six-shooter. A burly man with a very bushy beard stood there scowling at him and covering him. The fellow stared, then broke into a laugh.

"Where in hell did you come from? What are you doing out here without coat and hat and with that damn thing on your head?"

"Well, I'm not an officer of the law," Hawke replied solemnly. "And I'm not looking for any. Are you?"

The other laughed again. He didn't seem particularly belligerent. "Not so you could notice it. On the dodge, eh? What have you been doing?"

Hawke's solemnity became abysmal. "Oh, I'm bad medicine. I killed a sheepman down Rock Creek way. And I jumped the deputy sheriff while we were laying over last night at the stage station on the Big Sandy."

If the man suspected that Hawke was "stringing him" and playing for time in an attempt to create an opportunity to get the drop on him, he didn't show it. His laughter vanished in a suspicious scowl. "Then what was you doing standing here giving our camp a good looking over?"

"Oh, just sizing up the layout," Hawke returned blandly, "to make certain it wasn't a posse on my trail."

The man's suspicion did not decrease, nor did the gun in his hand waver. Hawke cursed the luck that armed him only with a rifle. "What did you shoot up the sheepman for?" the man demanded. "And it seems to me I've heard that officers put bracelets on their prisoners, especially killers."

Hawke shrugged. "The sheepman tried to beat me out of my wages and tried to run me off the place with a butcher knife. It ruffled my feelings. The sheriff didn't put any handcuffs on me when we went to bed. So I grabbed his rifle and tapped him over the head. This is the rifle." And Hawke started to swing the rifle up.

"Hold it!" barked the burly man. "Slick, ain't you? But not slick enough. You don't get the drop on me that way. Unless you want to stop lead right here and now, drop that rifle." Hawke knew when to temporize, which is one reason that he is still living. He dropped the rifle. The other man grunted in satisfaction. "Now mosey on down to the camp and we'll see what the other boys think about it."

Hawke walked down the hillside toward the camp, his debonair poise unshaken. The two men at the fire rose and stared at him. One of them, a very tall fellow with a long thin neck and a beak nose, chuckled and spoke to the man behind Hawke.

"Where'd you find it, Bull? And what is it?"

"Found him up there on the ridge sizing up the camp," Bull returned. "Says he's on the dodge for bumpin' off a sheepherder."

The third man, a short fellow whose shoulders were unusually broad and whose blue eyes were unusually hard, laughed. "I don't know as that's any crime. I'd like to bump off a few of 'em myself."

Evidently, the men were quite willing to make him at home and offer him a meal, but Hawke was not deceived. Bull had picked up the rifle, and all three of the men were heavily armed. Hawke realized fully that he was a prisoner, and if he wanted to get away with a whole hide he'd have to use his wits. His fabrication of the mythical and defunct sheepman had convinced them that he belonged to the same outlaw class as themselves, but they were wary and they were watching him. One of them prepared a meal for Bull and Hawke, and Hawke was hungry enough to relish it. At the same time he was watching intently for the first chance to escape from them and return to his own camp. When the meal was finished, Bull favored him with a sudden sharp look.

"We've got a ranch over this way, and we can use another hand. How'd you like a little job for a while, while you're on the hideout from that posse?"

Which was no invitation, Hawke knew well enough, but a thinly veiled command. "I guess you're running the show," he answered dryly.

"Yes, I guess so," Bull agreed. "We'd better get going."

They allowed him no opportunity to get any distance from them, but mounted him on a horse and kept him efficiently guarded. He was by this time certain they were rustlers, and that the horses were stolen. They traveled north, driving the horses ahead of them. They had given Travis a chunky bay without saddle or bridle, and only a hackamore to guide his mount. He scrutinized the horses and saw that no two of the branded ones bore the same brand, and several of them were not branded at all. The manner of the men was furtive, and they took care to leave as little trail as possible, keeping to rocky ridges whenever they could. Frequently during the journey they paused on convenient elevations to scrutinize the back trail. Horse thieves and no mistake.

It was dusk when they reached their objective, a large clearing littered with buildings and corrals. One of the men dismounted and let down the bars. The others drove the horses inside. As the rest of them dismounted, a big man with a heavy black beard emerged from the log house and came swiftly toward them. He glanced at the horses, then his gaze centered on Hawke Travis. He turned to the tall man with the beak nose.

"Where'd you get this, Jake? Who in hell is he?"

"Don't ask me," Jake returned, grinning and shrugging his lean shoulders. "Name it and you can have it. We found it down by the main trail: thought maybe you could use him."

In a few words the black-bearded man was apprised of Hawke's capture and of the tale he had told of killing a sheepman and eluding the sheriff. The man with the black beard was named Dobson, Hawke learned. As Jake finished his explanation, Dobson smiled. "Oh, we can use him all right. How many did you get this time?"

"Only sixteen," Jake answered, and swore roundly. "That damned Lander sheriff and some deputies from Kemmerrer have been watching the trail pretty close. Anyway, these will grade better than the last bunch."

They ignored Hawke's presence, and if he had needed any proof, more than his perceptions gave him, that these men were horse thieves, he had it in those words. The other men unsaddled the horses they had been riding, and they all trooped toward the house, carelessly but very pointedly keeping Hawke surrounded. The house was rather a rude affair, manifestly occupied only by men and littered abominably. The men gathered in the living room, and after some desultory conversation Hawke remarked to Dobson that he was tired and would like to roll in, if Dobson would show him to a bunk. Dobson eyed him with an openly suspicious gaze, but finally concluded that there was nothing in the request to indicate any hidden intent. He rose from his seat.

"Sure," he replied. "In early and up early. We've got plenty of work to do tomorrow. Follow me — what's your name?"

Hawke's eyes met his, bland and unreadable. "Anything you want to make it. How would Jones do, for a while?"

"Awful common," Dobson retorted, a smile quirking the corner of his mouth. Dobson is a fictitious name. Dobson is still living and would prefer that.

"Doesn't show much ingenuity on my part, does it?" Hawke agreed with Dobson's unspoken inference. "I'm too lazy to think tonight. We'll let Jones stick. Take it or leave it."

"Suits me." Dobson chuckled as he led Hawke across the room, out of it and across an open gallery literally heaped with old saddles, bridles, discarded boots and a dozen other things, and finally brought up in the bunk-room. This was no better than the rest of the house. It contained four pole bunks, and each bunk was furnished with a mat of hay to do duty for a mattress. Dobson waved a hand toward a lower bunk. "You can pile in there—Jones. But don't go to walkin' in your sleep—or you may stop lead."

Hawke made no reply, but seated himself on the edge of the bunk and began to remove his boots as if he were very eager indeed literally to "hit the hay." Dobson departed, carrying with him the candle he had used to light the way. Very promptly, Hawke followed in his sock feet. He slipped along the wall running between the gallery and the living room until he found a crack through the chinking. There he paused and peered into the room through the crack. The others were still sitting around the rough board table and Dobson had rejoined them. There was no light in the room but candlelight, as several candles were burning, stuck about here and there, and Hawke could see all of the men clearly. Dobson rolled himself a cigaret, lighted it at one of the candle flames, and turned to Jake with a scowl.

"What the hell do you mean by bringin' that hombre up here? I don't like his looks."

"Neither do I, but we had to bring him. He saw us with the horses, you poor fool," Jake answered, his words heated by resentment at the reproof. "He butted in on us just as we was ready to start. We didn't dare turn him loose. How the hell do we know who he is? Might be some dick or other, or some smart deputy. Some of them guys are pretty damn slick."

Dobson grunted and scowled. "I've kinda got an idea he may be a stock inspector. I'm damn sure I don't believe none of that song and dance about him bumpin' off that sheepherder and jumpin' the sheriff. Well, he's here, so we might as well make use of him. I'll get him busy on the hay."

Another of the men, the third one of those who had captured Hawke, a man called Harry, here interrupted. "Aw, to hell with the hay!" he snapped. "It won't be worth more than a measly hundred. I'm sick of this penny-ante game. I make a move that we tackle something worth while, the Overland, maybe. We oughta git enough out of that safe in the express car to put the whole gang on Easy Street."

"Ye-ah?" Dobson sneered openly. "And we might get the hell shot out of us by some of them extra guards they put over big shipments, too!

Nothing doing. That's too risky for me. Besides, I won't be ready to pull my freight before next summer. And I got to get even with that Wind River outfit—if it takes me five years."

Bull interrupted with a placating and diplomatic observation. "That *was* a rotten deal they handed you, Dobson. Maybe I'll ride with you when you cross the range. But meantime, we've got to think of our hides. I've got an idea; one reason I brought that guy along today. If any of the officers show up while we're waiting for the brands to heal, we can duck out and leave him to pay the freight."

Jake, he of the beak nose, also seemed to sense the advisability of placating Dobson and Harry. If Harry wanted to go after bigger game, it might be well to fall in with him. Harry was reckless, selfish and eternally restless. Jake addressed him with judicious gravity. "What's the matter with you and me sliding along and doing some business, Harry? The rest of 'em won't be doing much here but make hay and wait for the brands to heal. You and me might pull something down at Miners' Delight or Atlantic City. Or we oughta make a pretty good haul off the Lander stage."

Harry nodded, instantly approving and interested. "Sure suits me, Jake. Let's roll in. We been on the go for more'n a week, and I'm sleepy."

Hawke decided that it was time for him to quit his post of observation. He had learned plenty concerning this crew. He made his way back to the bunk assigned him by Dobson, and when the other men entered the bunk-room a few moments later he was apparently sound asleep.

After breakfast the next morning, Dobson told him he had changed his mind about having him help with the hay. Hawke listened, his face expressionless, as Dobson went on to say that the morning's work would be digging post holes for a fence. Hawke offered no remarks and no objections. He knew the full danger of his position, and he knew too that he would get out of it, in his own way. Dobson got a spade from the blacksmith shop and led the way to the upper end of the clearing where a line of posts was strung along the ground.

"Dig a line of post holes acrost this end," he commanded, tendering Hawke the spade. "Got to have a better fence than that brush one." He turned away without waiting for Hawke to speak, and strode rapidly back to the house.

Hawke proceeded to dig a post hole or two, keeping a sharp lookout on the house. Dobson reappeared shortly, carrying his rifle. With him were Jake and Harry, also carrying rifles in addition to their six-shooters. The three proceeded at a swift pace to the lower end of the clearing and disappeared into the brush and timber.

Hawke frowned and considered. It looked like a beautiful chance for escape. Seemingly all he had to do was walk away. He knew better. It was too easy. Bull was watching him from some concealed place, ready to drop him should he make the least suspicious move. Even if he were not being watched, Hawke had neither the inclination nor the folly to slip away afoot and unarmed. When he went, he was going right! Seemingly oblivious to anything about him, he bent his efforts on the digging, but he was in reality keeping close observation on his surroundings. The rustlers did not return till noon, and nothing occurred, save that Hawke dug a couple of post holes. After the noon meal, during which the others were markedly glum and silent, Hawke returned to his work. He hadn't been digging ten minutes when he heard a familiar whistle from beyond the brush fence above the line of posts. He straightened deliberately and turned his head.

"You devil!" he said in an undertone. "You've been slow."

The amused chuckle of Joe Towers answered him. "Well, how'd I know you was gonna chase up here to hell and gone just to git a job diggin' post holes? What kind of an outfit is this any-way?"

"Horse thieves," Hawke answered laconically. "I followed the deer—"

"Oh, I can read sign," Joe interrupted. "And you run into a band of rustlers and they stuck you on a horse and brought you up here. I followed when you didn't show up, and when I saw what had happened I fanned the breeze back to camp. Got me a camp about a mile down here to the west now. Your horse and stuff's there. Got your six-gun with me. Want it?"

Hawke shook his head. "Not right this minute, idiot. Shove it under that log sticking through the brush fence. I'll get it later. These guys took the horses down somewhere below the clearing, to brand 'em. Not far, I'd judge. You better beat it back to your camp till they take the horses up to the Basin. Then I'll make my getaway. Keep a lookout for me. I'll probably be with you about this time tomorrow."

But Hawke found himself foiled in his intent the next day. Dobson persistently remained with him, helping him set the posts. Bull left early that morning, and Jake and Harry shortly followed him. Hawke guessed that they had gone to drive the horses up into the Basin, and that Jake and Harry would probably go on to make their raid on the stage, leaving Bull to return alone. Since the day passed, with no possible opportunity arising for his escape, Hawke determined to leave as soon after nightfall as possible, to retrieve his gun from under the log and join Joe. But even that plan was shattered by Dobson. After the evening meal, as Hawke started for the bunk-room, Dobson caught his arm and motioned toward two bunks in a corner of the living room.

"You'll sleep there after this, hombre," Dobson commanded. "Can't afford to take chances on leavin' you escape at this stage of the game." And he grinned maliciously, as if he had read that intent in Hawke's mind.

Hawke made no reply, but strolled over to the bunk indicated and began to remove his boots. None of the others had as yet returned, and Dobson evidently was bent on keeping an extra close watch on the prisoner. The need for escape, and quick escape, had become imperative. Hawke had been listening to every scrap of conversation he could possibly overhear, and he had learned that they had no intention of letting him get away alive. They feared he might report them to the officers. Regardless of the fact that he had represented himself as one as chary of the law as they, they trusted no man with their affairs. Hawke had run into them and forced them to bring him to their camp—their version—and therefore Hawke must be put out of the way. At which thought, Hawke grinned scornfully to himself and pretended to go quickly to sleep, pretended to be exhausted from the terrific labor of digging a few post holes.

Presently Dobson blew out the two candles he had burning on the table and got into the other bunk, which was above the one in which Hawke lay with closed eyes and alert brain. Dobson did not go to sleep soon. The log in the fireplace burned down, the room was almost in darkness, before a slight snoring breath from the upper bunk told Hawke that Dobson at last slept.

Hawke cautiously shoved back the covers and swung his legs to the floor, drew on his trousers and picked up his boots, intending to slip out in his sock feet to avoid making the least sound. But Dobson was not asleep on the job. Behind him Hawke heard the ominous click of a raised hammer, the hammer of a gun, and Dobson's voice snapped at him.

"That's far enough, hombre. I can see you good enough to drop you. Stand right there till I light a candle." The puncheon floor shook as he dropped to it from his bunk. He scratched a match and touched the flame to the wick of a candle he had at hand. "I been waitin' just for some such move —Jones," he said, with heavy sarcasm. "Stick your hands behint you. You'll git no more chance to go even this far. Put 'em behint you, quick!"

Hawke cursed, but he obeyed. Dobson had him covered with a cocked gun and would not hesitate to shoot. He tied Hawke's wrists and started to voice a command. He had brought the candle with him and had placed it on the table.

"Now move over—" But he got no further.

In back of Dobson, the window glass crashed and the muzzle of a Colt was thrust through the shattered pane. Dobson whirled, his eyes widening.

"What say *you* stick 'em up for a change?" drawled the voice of Joe Towers. "And drop that gun on the table."

Dobson obeyed, fuming, but neatly caught. Towers chuckled. "That's the ticket, hombre. Now stand hitched till I crawl in through the windah."

"Wait!" Hawke commanded sharply. "I'll back up to the window and you cut this hogging string."

Joe grunted assent, and Hawke backed slowly, careful not to get between Towers and Dobson. Dobson suddenly lowered both hands and swept the candle from the table, and at the same time snatched at his gun. As he saw Dobson's hands start downward, Hawke leaped, lowering his head and driving it into Dobson's side. There was terrific force behind that plunge, and Dobson went to the floor, striking on his back. His breath was knocked out of him. Towers darted around the house and in through the door, slashed Hawke's bonds and relighted the candle, replacing it on the table. Hawke bent over Dobson.

"I'll put you on your bunk till you get your wind back," he said.

Dobson snorted. "Wind—back! You broke a rib —or two." He groaned with the pain of returning breath. "You—you *sure* broke—a rib."

"Sorry," Hawke snapped. "But this is war. Be good and you won't get hurt. Joe, poke up the fire and hand over that bottle of Mustang Liniment up there on the shelf. This guy think's he's killed."

In a short time Dobson was sitting on the edge of the lower bunk, smoking a cigaret, rubbing his side, and scowling curiously at Hawke. "Well, why don't you beat it? You got my gun, and there ain't nobody here to stop you. And what you gonna do with me?"

"Why, let you alone, of course," Hawke returned. "And we're certainly going to beat it. As soon as the coast's clear."

Dobson's gaze instantly turned suspicious. "What do you mean by that?"

"I know," Hawke retorted dryly. "But I'm not telling. Perhaps I choose to stay here and take the rest of them into camp."

Dobson's laugh rose at that, deriding. Hawke ignored him; he himself knew why he did not immediately walk out. Second thought had urged him not to make his escape *too* soon. Jake and Harry were intending to rob some stage or a train, it was impossible to conjecture what kind of mess they might stir up. If Hawke took Joe and lit out now, he might be playing into their hands, might be making it possible, even more, might be making it convenient, for them to set a trap and so lay circumstantial evidence that the authorities would blame Hawke and Joe for the robbery. Hawke considered that it was bad enough to be trailed for what he had done, without being saddled with something of which he was not guilty. He was determined not to leave until he was certain nothing of that kind was left behind him, until he had assured himself that they would not so maneuver as to make him "pay the freight," as Bull had expressed it. And since Dobson was unaware of his knowledge of the thing Harry and Jake contemplated, since he had heard it when he was eavesdropping, Dobson could see no reason, of course, for Hawke's remaining any longer.

Something of the same thing was in Joe Towers' mind. He gazed at Hawke with veiled curiosity, but he asked no questions. He knew Hawke's caution, and that was enough. The three stayed in the house all night, and Hawke and Joe planned activities with serene disregard of Dobson's presence. Hawke said that Joe should stay and keep an eye on Dobson, the next morning, while he went out to round up Bull, who would be somewhere with the horses. Joe was agreeable to anything that promised action. Dobson sneered at them; yes, they'd get Bull! He was a good prophet. Hawke did get Bull.

At sundown the next day, Dobson and Joe saw Hawke returning from his foray. Ahead of him, Hawke drove the rustled horses, and immediately preceding him rode Bull, slumped forward in his saddle. Joe, eager to hear what had happened, herded Dobson out onto the narrow porch. Hawke turned the horses into the corral, put up the bars and brought his prisoner to the house. Bull was so weak from loss of blood that Hawke was forced to all but carry him; his right arm was bared to the shoulder, the sleeve cut away. A bloody bandage was around the arm and a tourniquet was twisted tightly above the elbow. Evidently, Hawke hadn't got him without a little grim persuasion.

It transpired that Bull had attempted to go for his gun when Hawke rode up and demanded that he surrender. They got him into the house, and Bull demanded his "snake bite remedy." It was given to him, a quart bottle of Old Crow whiskey. He wasn't in a particularly belligerent mood, he had been suffering intensely and the fight was taken out of him. Joe kept a general eye on things while Hawke and Dobson washed and dressed the wounded arm. The bullet had caused a serious wound, had grazed the bone. Hawke had his own particular ideas about dressing that wound. Before the bandage was put on, he sent Joe out with a lantern. It had grown dark by now. He told Joe to scrape from some of the big pines about the house a quantity of pitch and bring it to him. He spread the pitch thickly over the wound and bound the arm from wrist to elbow.

Bull was entirely glad to lie back on the bunk in the corner and close his eyes. As far as causing any particular trouble was concerned, Bull was out of the running. He was exhausted and depleted enough to desire only opportunity to rest and recuperate, and fight his pain with Old Crow. Too, any reckless movement might start the deep wound bleeding again.

The next thing was a meal, and Joe got that for all of them. Bull refused to eat, he had no appetite. The others ate heartily, and Joe and Dobson sat back smoking. Hawke very seldom smoked. Dobson attempted to learn the reason for Hawke's insistence on remaining at the ranch.

"You've got yourself into a jackpot," he predicted darkly. "You think Jake and Harry are going to sit here twiddling their thumbs while you run off them horses?"

Hawke made no reply. He saw no reason for saying that he had no intention of saddling himself with a herd of stolen horses, just as he saw no reason for explaining that he had brought the horses back lest they, if turned loose, should strike for home and so lead officers to the hangout. So he said nothing at all. Harry and Jake were due to show up any time. After a moment of silent thinking, he turned to Dobson.

"It looks to me like you're in a jackpot yourself. Joe followed the trail of those horses easily. Sheriff Starr might do the same."

Dobson started violently. "He followed the trail of the horses? What did them damn fools mean leaving a trail? The sheriff don't need much of an excuse to come romping up here. I'd better pull my freight."

"What's your hurry?" The caustic question came from the doorway. Harry had stepped silently into sight, Jake at his shoulder. Harry shot a hostile glance at Hawke, who sat with both elbows on the table, coolly returning the look. "Been raisin' hell, ain't you?" he remarked. "Well, don't move. Jake, slip in and take their hardware and tie 'em up."

Hawke thought quickly, but still made no reply. Resistance would be worse than useless. Harry had stepped into the open door with both guns cocked, he had the drop on them. Jake disarmed Joe and took from Hawke the gun Hawke had taken from Dobson. Jake made one mistake. Hawke was wearing Dobson's gun and belt. After Jake had tied him, he was still wearing a gun the presence of which was unknown to Jake, his own forty-four, inside the waistband of his trousers under his vest. Jake passed the confiscated guns to Harry, and Harry ordered the prisoners to sit on a bench along the wall.

"What brought you back so quick?" Dobson inquired.

"Got word from the station tender at the Big Sandy that the damn officers was layin' for us," Harry explained briefly, but he shifted his gaze, and eyes as keen as Hawke's saw that he was lying. He and Jake both were thoroughly angered at seeing Bull so badly wounded. They warmed over what was left of the supper, and when they ate it they both made another mistake, for, in their assurance that Hawke and Joe were efficiently subdued, they sat down to their meal with their backs turned toward their prisoners. Hawke lost no time in taking advantage of that. He nudged Joe with his knee, moved close and partly turned his back. Joe was quick, shrewd and daring. He reached out with his bound hands and untied the rope knotted around Hawke's wrists. Before Jake and Harry had finished their meal, both Joe and Hawke were free of their bonds.

There was nothing to evidence the fact. They both sat motionless on the bench, waiting an opportunity. As Harry gulped the last of his coffee, he rose from the table, put on his hat and spoke to Jake. "Guess I'll go and rub down my cayuse. He was all het up. Yours will need some rubbing, too."

Jake nodded. "I'll attend to him after a bit. No rush."

With a nod of understanding, Harry went out. Watching them intently, alive to every expression and tone, Hawke sensed the fact that Harry's going out to rub down his horse was merely a ruse. He intended something entirely different, and Jake knew what it was. There was some kind of secret understanding between them. Jake waited a few moments at the table, after Harry had gone, then sat suddenly erect, his eyes on the door, sprang abruptly to his feet, caught up his hat and spoke to Dobson.

"I'm going out to attend to my horse," he explained, with some haste and a good deal of uneasiness. "You keep your eyes on these two hombres till I get back." Without waiting for Dobson's answer he hurried out and slammed the door behind him.

In the same split second, Hawke was on his feet, his Colt out and covering Dobson. Dobson stared, and Hawke said sharply: "You be good."

Dobson grinned dryly. "Sure I'll be good. I ain't a damn fool. You're too damn sudden and unexpected for me."

"Here too, Pete," Bull put in from his bunk in the corner. "Me, I wouldn't wish any more pie. Besides, seems to me Jake and Harry's acting damn funny."

Hawke said nothing to that. He kept Dobson covered while Joe again removed Dobson's gun from its owner's possession. Bull offered an ironical warning:

"Better not try to stick up Jake and Harry, hombre. Lead's liable to fly kinda permiscuous. They're tough babies."

"Yeh," Dobson approved. "Bull's right. Better bend a six-shooter over their heads."

Hawke smiled. The shoe was on the other foot, now. Dobson and Bull had begun to sense that they were being double-crossed. A silence fell over the room as they waited for the other two to return. Suddenly there came the sound of feet running swiftly toward the house from the corral. Hawke was waiting when Jake burst in the doorway, and brought the barrel of his forty-four Colt down heavily on Jake's head. Unfortunately, the blow was not true. The barrel glanced down the right side of Jake's head and face, knocking off his hat. Jake grunted in pain and surprise, and acted with a quickness that was automatic. He whirled and threw both arms around Hawke in a bear-like hug.

Hawke raised his right knee and drove it into Jake's groin. Jake literally howled, and relaxed his grip. Hawke jerked free, and struck again with the Colt. He missed Jake's head and the blow descended upon the rustler's shoulder. Jake went berserk. With a sound very much like a roar, he advanced on Hawke with flailing fists. In the scuffle to avoid again being caught in Jake's bear grip, Hawke lost his gun. He dodged around the plank table, and Jake pursued him. Hawke dodged back, and managed to send a telling blow to Jake's stomach. In the meantime, Joe had picked up Dobson's rifle. As Jake halted a moment, winded and stopped by the stomach blow, Joe brought the Winchester down squarely on his head. Jake wilted to the floor, effectually silenced and stilled. Hawke snatched up his Colt, ordering Joe to shut the door while he tied Jake.

There ensued another wait; for Harry. It was short-lived. It lasted only till Jake returned to consciousness and struggled to a sitting position.

"You're wasting time," he advised them sourly. "Harry's pulled his freight."

"What are you trying to tell us?" Hawke demanded.

"What I said," Jake snapped. "He's pulled out, leaving the rest of us to pay the freight. He took his pick of the horses, and I came tearing in here to get you to go with me and stop him. And see what you done."

Hawke eyed him intently. "Just why has he pulled his freight?"

"Because he's got sixteen thousand dollars worth of gold dust in his saddlebags," Jake answered. "And he didn't want to divide it with me."

"It all becomes very clear." Hawke frowned, his eyes hardening. "The two of you were figuring on double-crossing Dobson and Bull. I'll wager you left a trail up here that the sheriff could follow in the dark. And Harry goes you one better. Serves you right. What are you going to do, Dobson?"

Dobson shrugged. "Head for the Hole-in-the-Wall, I reckon, and do it damn quick."

With surly resentment at Harry in his voice and face, Jake approved the move. Bull was worried.

"But what about me?" he demanded. "I'm kinda bashful when it comes to meetin' women and sheriffs."

"Keep your shirt on and stand pat," Hawke advised him. "They can't prove that you had anything to do with rustling the horses, and, if it will do you any good, I can testify that you weren't with Harry and Jake when they robbed the stage. I didn't see you rustle any horses. You can't stand much traveling right now. You'd better hole up somewhere and keep quiet. Joe and I are off for Lander."

Whether or not Dobson and Jake safely reached the Hole-in-the-Wall, Hawke never knew. At least, they were never brought to trial for the robbery of the stage and for the rustling. They escaped some way. Nor did he know what became of Bull. He was not taken by the authorities. That is one stage robbery that remained a mystery unsolved. Hawke and Joe took a small supply of grub from the ranch and went on to Lander.

V

Before they reached Lander, they turned loose the horses they were riding and entered the town afoot. Lander was quiet, as far as they were concerned. It was the county seat, but it was a small town. There were not more than a dozen establishments of business in it at that time. There was no work of any consequence, unless a man wanted a job punching cows on a near-by ranch. It was, however, a good business town, Lander, since it was the chief trading post of a vast territory. Joe stayed in Lander for a few days, then went on. It was too quiet for him. Hawke remained.

Hawke's experiences had been wide. He had at one time spent over a year in a law office and had tried cases before the Justice of the Peace court, for which he needed no diploma. He knew something of law. So the gunman, thinking wisely that a little quietude might be good for his health, decided to hang out a shingle and see what he could do in the law business.

He had his office in an upstairs front room of one of the two hotels in Lander. It was the main hotel, where the stage stopped.

One instance will be enough to show the delicious spiciness of his activities as a lawyer.

There was in Lander a big man whose name must remain out of this. He was a gambler, a gunman, a business man, a rancher. He was about everything. We'll call him Blondy, because nobody ever did. There was another man who frequented Lander, whose name was Three-Fingered Jackson. This Jackson was a gunman of no mean ability, also, and was very justly feared. Hawke had no use for him. He wasn't considerate of his horses, one thing that would raise Hawke's ire perhaps a little more quickly than anything else. One time Jackson left his horses to stand out in the street all night. It was cold weather, and Hawke took the horses over to the livery stable. The next morning, Jackson came blustering around and demanded to know who the hell had been monkeying with his horses and putting them in the livery stable.

"I did it," Hawke told him quietly. "What are you going to do about it?"

Jackson measured Hawke with his eyes, and growled that he "guessed he wasn't going to do anything about it." He had learned who put up his horses, and he had learned that Hawke Travis was not afraid of him.

There were three saloons in Lander. One of them was run by Pete Peralto, the constable. Blondy and Three-Fingered Jackson got into an argument in Peralto's saloon. Blondy carried two guns, inside the waistband of his trousers. Which wasn't so unusual. But—he carried them in back,

99

which *was* unusual. That night Pete Peralto's saloon was crowded. Jackson and Blondy raised a very heated quarrel. It is to be regretted that the cause of that quarrel cannot be repeated, it savors so richly of the Old West, but Blondy is living. He is one of those fortunate men on whose land oil was found. He is well-to-do today, and very probably would strenuously object to his name and the cause of that quarrel being made public. A woman figured in the question. Suffice it to say that they quarreled.

Blondy drew both guns and fired on Three-Fingered Jackson. He did not shoot to kill, did not want to kill, desired merely to frighten Jackson.

The saloon was in an uproar instantly, people running in every direction; out both doors and even through the windows they went. Hawke calmly stepped behind the stove. It wasn't his quarrel, and he had no desire to stop a stray bullet. He was, admirably, discreet. Another reason that he's still living. Jackson fell to the floor. He thought he was killed, but he had merely a scratch on the neck.

Blondy was promptly arrested and arraigned before the Justice of the Peace, and Hawke Travis was appointed prosecutor. The whole trial was a farce, and Hawke knew it. The Justice of the Peace had no right to try Blondy, since he was limited to petty cases. This was a felony case and should have gone before the District Court. But it didn't. It was tried before the Justice, Hawke prosecuting—and Blondy was acquitted.

Such were the law cases of the gunman-lawyer. There wasn't much to be made in such procedure. I mentioned before the three saloons in the town. In all of them various gambling games were running. Hawke decided to do a little gambling on the side. He had played many a game; the things his slim, hard fingers could do with a pack of cards were a living demonstration of the assertion that the quickness of the hand deceives the eye. He had put that ability to work before, and now he put it into practice again. But neither prosecuting fellow gunmen nor expert juggling of cards realized the returns Hawke deemed commensurate with the effort expended. Most of the time he was broke, stony. He drifted into close association with several crooks who had been stranded in the town. These men had been duly impressed by Hawke's lack of fear of the notorious Three-Fingered Jackson. It wasn't long till Hawke was considered tacit leader of the band. They began looking about for some way of making easy money.

Hawke proposed that they rob the local bank. The bank was a one-man affair. No clerks were hired by the Frenchman who ran it. Some of the other men in the band objected to this robbery, explaining that the getaway would be difficult. None of them had a horse or money to buy one.

The nearest railway was sixty-five miles from Lander. Little town of Lander, then. Bigger town of Lander, now, sitting calmly in the Wind River country of Wyoming, modernized and sedate. I wonder if she remembers the echo of guns and the smell of powder? She had her days. One of them was about to break.

When the other men vetoed Hawke's suggestion to rob the bank, another member of the gang offered his idea. He was an ex-stage driver who was called Smoky and his idea was to rob the Chinese laundry. The laundry had been doing a good business for several years; it was believed that the Chinese did not bank his money. It appeared that robbing the laundry might be a profitable move.

This time it was Hawke who objected; for still another of the men had something to offer. This fellow was a snaky-eyed ex-convict. He was on terms of too friendly a character with Sheriff Starr to suit Hawke. The ex-convict proposed that the gang meet in a vacant house to talk over his plan for robbing the big general store; he thought it looked better than either the laundry or the bank. Hawke went to the empty house, wary and suspicious. He suddenly suspected a trap, because of the actions of the ex-convict. At the empty house, Hawke decided definitely that something was wrong with the whole business. If they were so fearful of being able to make a getaway, why did they veto the robbery he suggested, and yet immediately suggest another themselves? Fully convinced that they were trying to trap him, Hawke refused to have anything more to do with the gang.

He hadn't a friend among them, save Smoky. Smoky, he was certain, was not in league with the others. Smoky had not objected to robbing the bank and had not agreed in general with the others at all. Hawke's trust narrowed down to Smoky, and the two joined forces. They talked further of robbing the laundry, but finally gave it up. They decided to leave Lander. They went to Washakie, where they hoped to get a job in a wood camp, cutting wood for the Arapahoe Indian Agency.

Pete Peralto, the constable from Lander, followed them to Washakie and arrested them. Someone had robbed the Chinese laundry, and Hawke and Smoky were considered guilty of the felony. They were astounded, but made no move to resist Pete.

Hawke rather liked Pete. Constable Pete had nerve, Hawke says. Hawke once saw the constable stride out into the main street of Lander and confront a drunken gunman who was bent upon shooting up the town. Pete didn't even so much as draw his revolver. He walked up to the belligerent and drunken roisterer and took his guns away from him. Wild and woolly days? Rather! Hawke has seen the time when he sat in a poker game, and cowpunchers in hilarious spirits rode their horses into the saloon, whooping and yelling, and shooting through the top of the table at which Hawke played. In those hectic days, Pete Peralto was considered a nervy guy. It was anything but discreet to oppose him. Hawke and Smoky returned with him to Lander.

Arrived there, they found all defense useless. The ex-convict had set the trap, and sprung it. Sheriff Starr testified that he had found the tracks of Hawke's boots in the fresh snow about the wash house, and it would not have been easy to convince him that Hawke's feet were not within the boots when the tracks were made. The ex-convict swore that Hawke and Smoky had been planning with two or three other men to rob the Chinese laundry. Several hundred dollars had been taken. After the preliminary hearing before Judge Richardson, Hawke and Smoky were bound over to the next term of court. They found themselves in the jail at Lander, incarcerated for a robbery they had planned but had not committed.

The jail stood by itself some distance from the edge of the town. It was in charge of an elderly man whom everybody called Dad. Escape from the jail seemed to present no great difficulty, and Hawke and Smoky began considering the best and surest way of leaving Lander behind. There was much *to* consider. True, the escape from the building itself was easy enough, but that once

accomplished, difficulties *did* present themselves. The trial and the formalities had taken
time, the season was advanced, it was extremely
cold and the ground was covered by a good foot
of snow. Consider the facts that it was sixty-five
miles to the nearest railroad, that the weather was
bitterly cold, that neither man would have a horse
or opportunity to get one, that snow is an excellent medium for taking beautifully clear tracks,
and the difficulties at once become apparent.

These things, however, did not stop Hawke and
Smoky. The confinement in the jail was irksome,
but that was the smallest part of it. The thing that
drove them to attempt an escape, and a getaway
that seemed impossible, was the fear of being sent
to the Laramie penitentiary for two or three years.
The evidence was too strong against them to
allow of any chance for acquittal. Their only possible way of evading the penitentiary was to
escape from the Lander jail and keep going. There
were two other prisoners in the jail, accused of
rustling, and Hawke invited them to join in the jail
break. The rustlers flatly refused. They frankly
admitted that they preferred winter in the warm
jail, with nothing to do but eat good grub and play
cards with Dad. The old jailer was genial and a
good cook. Besides, the other two prisoners predicted that such an attempt was insane and utterly
hopeless. If the jail-breakers were not caught and
brought back, they would be frozen to death.

Deaf to all such arguments, seeing the penitentiary looming, Hawke and Smoky completed their plans. Most pertinent was the fact that after all they *hadn't* robbed the Chinese. The days passed and the cold grew more intense, but still they put off the escape, waiting for a snowstorm that would cover their tracks and aid in their evasion of pursuers. Then something occurred to force Hawke's hand. Dad had taken Hawke to the barber shop for a badly needed haircut. As they were returning, and after they had passed the last house on the way to the jail, Dad paused in the trail and eyed Hawke with something hidden and suggestive in his gaze.

"I got a tip today that might interest you, Hawke. But for God's sake keep it under your hat. Atkins says they're thinking of sending you and Smoky down to Rawlins." Starr's term was done, Atkins was now sheriff. "He thinks you're a desperate hombre, and believes you've been at the head of most of the deviltry pulled off in this country lately. I reckon you savvy what that transfer means. That Laramie pen ain't no health resort, you won't have a chance in the world to get away from there. Now's the time to talk turkey, if you got anything to say about the money you taken from that Chink and planted somewhere about town."

Hawke's first impulse was to deny any complicity in the robbery and any knowledge of the whereabout of the money, as he had denied both many times before. Then it suddenly ocurred to him that Dad didn't believe in his innocence and wouldn't believe in it, and that the old fellow had some cogent reason for bringing up the subject at this timc and place. With the intent of sounding the jailer's motive, Hawke asked:

"What is there in it for me if I tell you where to find that cache?"

The jailer's eyes sparkled a bit, and in a few seconds Hawke had full information. If he would produce the cash stolen from the laundry, and split it with Dad, Dad had planned a neat escape. The old fellow's idea was that, after the money was divided between him and Hawke, he would take Hawke to the barber shop. On the way back to the jail, Hawke was to muss him up a bit and leave him lying in the snow. When Hawke had had sufficient time to get away, Dad would "regain consciousness" and raise a hue and cry because his prisoner had escaped.

But when Hawke reminded Dad that Smoky was in on it make or break, the old man refused flatly to have anything to do with it if the money had to be divided three ways, and ordered Hawke to proceed to the jail. Hawke shrugged and grinned to himself. He had no money to divide, but he had been interested in the processes of Dad's mind. Also, Dad's desire to get some of the money had been the cause of Hawke's acquiring valuable information. If Sheriff Atkins contemplated moving him and Smoky to Rawlins, it was indeed time to act. He told Smoky the moment he could get a word aside with him. They decided to wait no longer, regardless of the weather, and to break jail the next day.

Every day Dad left his prisoners locked in the main room at the jail, and went to the butcher shop and store for food supplies. It was for this trip Hawke and Smoky waited the next day. The sky was clouded over and it was nearly dark when Dad finally took his basket and went. Immediately Hawke and Smoky became very busy, while the other two prisoners sat and watched with amused interest.

The first thing the two jail-breakers did was to gather up all the cooked food they could carry. They stuffed it into their pockets and inside the fronts of their flannel shirts. They drained heavily Dad's supply of sulphur matches and coffee. Hawke whittled out a wooden pin, while Smoky was engaged in tightening the window sashes so securely that they could not be moved without a tool. Then they waited, watching through the windows, for Dad's return. His footsteps sounded, crunching in the snow, before he came into sight through the falling dusk. Hawke and Smoky hurried to take their positions, one on either side of the door. Dad fumbled at the lock, an old-fashioned padlock in the hasp outside the door, unlocked it, and the door swung inward.

As the jailer entered the room, Smoky and Hawke lunged at him together. They made no attempt to hurt him. It was sufficient to take him by surprise and send him sprawling on the plank floor among his groceries. Before he had time to recover himself and get on his feet, Hawke and Smoky had darted outside the jail. Hawke slammed shut the door, clamped the hasp over it, and into the staple protruding through the slot in the hasp he thrust the wooden pin he had whittled. He and Smoky were out of the jail, and Dad was locked inside with his prisoners, the windows wedged tight.

Hawke and Smoky went at a run across the bottom lying between the jail and a branch of Little Wind River. Before they reached the brush-lined stream, much noise arose from the jail behind them. Finding the windows wedged, Dad smashed out the glass with the barrel of his gun, began firing the revolver in the air and shouting at the top of his voice to attract attention. He couldn't get out of his own jail, but he was bent on arousing the town. Response was not long in coming. Hawke and Smoky paused at the edge of the timber and brush along the stream, to look back. Numerous figures, like dark moving blots against the snow, were racing from town toward the jail. The fugitives dashed on through the brush to the stream. They found the stream frozen over, and leaped onto the ice, racing downstream till they reached a low bridge spanning the ice-covered water at the crossing of the Rawlins Road.

They scrambled up on the bridge and went running down the road. The surface here was hard packed by wagons and teams, it would take no impression, bear no tell-tale tracks by which pursuers could trail the fugitives. They raced down this road until they reached a place where it crossed a sharp ridge. The winds had swept the ridge barren of snow. Hawke and Smoky turned eastward on the ridge, and followed it to the top of a low range. There they swung to another ridge which also had been denuded of snow by the wind. This ridge led them to another stream, running south, and here again they took to the ice. So they kept going all through the night.

In order to realize the daring of the two men in embarking upon this escape, and their bravery in persisting in it, several things should be noted. Their clothes were very thin; thin socks, thin underwear, thin summer suits, with flannel shirts as their only warm article of clothing, constituted their only protection against the weather. They had no overcoats to ward off the cutting cold, the wind and storm. They had no gloves, no fur caps with side flaps, to shield easily-frozen digits and ears. They had no overshoes to mitigate the wear on their thin shoes and to keep them dry. They had little food. True, they had taken all the cooked food Dad had in his cupboard, but it wasn't very much. There they were, two men in thin clothing, rushing into a wild region, braving snow and storm, and the thermometer was hanging around forty below zero.

During that first night they ate all their food, rendered ravenous by the bitter cold and the exertion of their travel. When morning came they had eaten the last crumb. They had been well fed in the jail, they were in good condition. They did not stop when daylight broke but continued steadily onward. The region was thinly settled, thus far they had seen but one ranch, and they went around that in a wide arc to evade being seen. Shortly after dawn they came upon a sheep camp, so situated that they were upon it before they realized that it was there.

It was too late then to escape observation. The sheep dogs instantly were raising a clamor and the sheepherder thrust his head through the door of the camp wagon. Hawke asked what chance there was of getting a meal. The herder replied that there was no chance whatever. He was very surly about it. He hadn't, he said, enough food for himself, the chuck wagon hadn't come around that month. He eyed them suspiciously and wanted to know what they were doing out there without overcoats and arctics. They pretended to be lost, to have strayed off the Rawlins Road.

The herder grunted, only half inclined to believe them, and directed them to the road. They went on, taking the direction he indicated, hurrying to get out of his sight.

Beyond his range of view, they turned east again on the first barren ridge that crossed their trail. As they started up the ridge, snow began falling. It was still falling when they paused at evening for the first time since leaving the jail. *That was one day without food.* They made their camp upon a flat where sage-brush grew, big sage-brush, much of it as high as their heads. They were tired now, feeling the rigor of their travel. They were very hungry.

They thought of the warning spoken by the rustlers in the jail at Lander. The danger of freezing to death was no mere figment of groundless fear. It was a very real danger. Their first concern was to prevent such a thing's happening. They built a huge sage-brush fire. When the snow was thawed in a circle, the ground comparatively warm and dry under the fire, they moved the fire over onto the snow and replenished it. They built another fire opposite this one, so that the bare ground where the fire had been was now between the two fires. On that warmed ground they sat and dozed. So they passed the night, snatching sleep and resting as much as they could, keeping their fires going, moving the fires and profiting by the warmth left in the ground. So they minimized the cold, though the snow continued to fall and the storm did not abate.

In the morning they trudged on. It was harder to travel now. They were becoming ever more ravenously hungry, their strength was failing in the cold and exertion more swiftly than it would have done under other conditions. Of the country into which they were traveling, they knew nothing save by hearsay. But they knew enough of it to be certain there was not likely to be a ranch within a hundred miles in the direction they were taking. They exerted themselves to renewed effort to combat the cold by activity as they tramped on. All day they traveled, growing desperately weary, seeing no signs of life, until evening brought them to a pass through a low range of mountains.

Here they found an old cabin. There was nothing in it, save a few empty cans scattered about, a fireplace and two bare bunks. But at least the cabin was snug, and protection against the cold. In front of the fireplace were scattered numerous old cigaret butts. Smoky picked them up and made cigarets of the tobacco in them, using some old paper he had in his pocket. He got a little comfort from the smoke, but Hawke did not smoke. There the two spent the night, with a roaring fire in the fireplace, and found the bare bunks at least warmer and drier than the bare ground. *That was two days without food.*

The next morning they went on again, noting in

passing several springs covered with a seepage of oil, as weary men will note trivial but unusual things. Again they traveled all day, and at the end of that day they paused on a low ridge and saw ahead of them the badly broken region of the Bad Lands. It did not look to be more than ten miles away, but they knew it was farther than that. It was a grim and forbidding country. They were wearing down now. *This was three days without food.* Their hunger and fatigue had become genuine torture. It seemed to them they could not go on unless they had something to put in their empty stomachs. But there was no opportunity of getting it. There were known to be herds of antelope in that region. They had not seen one antelope, not one living thing in the wild and barren stretch, save a few stray jackrabbits. Hawke had tried several times to get one with a rock, and failed.

The snow lay over everything. There was nothing at all that they could eat. They were in the Big Horn Basin, south of the Big Horn Range. There were no ranches to the north for many miles. East and north were the Bad Lands. To the south of them reared a high bluff, perhaps five hundred feet high. From the top of that bluff a mesa stretched away, rolling down to the country of the Sweetwater River. Around the Sweetwater, ranches were to be found. Behind them, to the west, was Lander.

Now, into this record come two strange happenings. Hawke cannot account for them. He only knows they happened. You can explain them away as you will, they still remain strange and significant events in that grim and heart-wrecking journey. The first of the two happenings was this; both men began to hear the sound of cow bells. It was not a jumbled and indeterminate sound, a mere ringing in the ears such as might be caused by exhaustion and hunger. It was the clear and unmistakable tinkle of cow bells. It seemed to be leading them toward a ranch where they might find shelter and food to keep them from perishing. Each man was fearful that the other might think he was growing light-headed if he mentioned hearing the bells, and each man kept it to himself. But they followed it, the sound of the cow bells, for four or five miles. Then they paused upon this low ridge from which they could see the Bad Lands.

Then for the first time one of them spoke of hearing the bells, and they stood gazing at each other with startled eyes when they learned that the sound had been clear to each of them alike. And now the sound was gone. Puzzled, feeling a little queer about it, they started on. Then the second strange thing happened.

Smoky stopped short and pointed. Get in your mind the exact terrain surrounding them. Straight ahead of them, due east, the Bad Lands began and ranged to the north, to the left. To the right, south, raised this high bluff. It had been running along to their right for many miles. Ahead, it swung in an arc to the east and merged with the Bad Lands. Due ahead of them a low ridge ran from the Bad Lands, straight across their path, and merged with the gullies at the base of the bluff to the right. It was to this ridge that Smoky pointed.

Along the ridge, coming from the Bad Lands, rode a horseman. Hawke nodded at the sight, his eyes lighted. To both of them came some renewed energy and endurance, for the presence of the rider promised a near place where shelter and food might be obtainable. They judged he must be a line rider from some ranch, and guessed that ranch was likely to be located along the base of the big bluff to the right. The puncher was going in that direction.

Smoky laughed aloud in relief. "Beefsteak and coffee for supper, old timer!" he exclaimed. Hawke sighed and felt a little sick at the stomach, in sheer relief. He hadn't realized how nearly done up he was until promise of rest and food was in sight.

They hurried on to the ridge down which the puncher was riding, intending to follow his tracks to the ranch. By the time they reached the ridge the rider had disappeared from sight. The ridge merged with a gulch at the foot of the bluff, a heavily timbered gulch, into which the rider had gone. They judged the ranch must be in that gulch. But when they reached the place where his tracks should have been, they stopped short, and blank amazement overspread their features, their eyes widened and stared in unbelief. No track was there. The snow stretched down over the ridge in a smooth, unbroken sheet. Nowhere was there the least sign of tracks either of man or beast. Smoky turned to Hawke, his eyes dazed with bewilderment.

"I'll be damned if that don't beat me! I'd a swore on a stack of Bibles that I seen that rider crossing this ridge. I *did* see him! I know I saw him. He was wearing a buffalo overcoat, and the snow was flying up in front of the cayuse's legs. Was that—was that what you saw?"

Hawke nodded slowly, staring down the ridge and then at Smoky. "Of course," he said, his voice sharpened by disappointment. That was the way he was dressed. And he had on a fur cap. More, the horse was a buckskin. What in God's name do you make of it? The fellow was here!" But he wasn't there, and there was no sign of his having been there, though it would have been impossible for anything to walk down that ridge and into that gulch without making heavy tracks in the snow.

Strange! Both men saw the horse and rider, both saw exactly the same things. A mirage? An hallucination of men rendered dizzy by exhaustion and hunger? So some people might assert. As I said before, even today Hawke has no explanation for it. I have my own belief regarding that occurrence. I prefer not to state it in so many words. But in these pertinent facts, to any person who has a faith that something beyond the ken of man protects and guides in hours of great extremity, my own belief must reveal itself.

These are the pertinent facts to which I allude. Hawke and Smoky stood there on the ridge, bewildered, heartsick and disappointed. They were very surely facing death. They must have food of some kind, and some manner of shelter, or they would die. Food they must have quickly, or they would never see the morning. In a wild country they did not know they had followed the sound of cow bells for four miles or more, thinking always that a ranch must be just ahead of them. Then the sound was gone, and this puncher came riding across the ridge ahead of them, by his very presence promising shelter and food, only to prove as incorporeal as a phantom.

They turned and looked at the gulch into which he had gone, and followed. There was no ranch in the gulch, not even an old line cabin. The gulch was littered with dead and down timber. To their right reared the high bluff, to their left was now the lower slope of the other side of the gulch. But—in that wild place they found the only food nature had to offer. There they found the first thing they could even consider edible. They found a thick growth of wild rose bushes. Protected largely from the whipping winds, the bushes were plentifully covered with the brilliant little red seed-pods we all know, meaty little pods with fat seeds in them. Rose pods with little fat seeds can be a banquet to men facing death through hunger and cold. They ate of the pods until their hunger was somewhat appeased.

The horseman had led them there, the horseman who was not. Figure it out for yourself. There is little doubt that those rose pods saved their lives that night. There is little doubt that, out in the open away from the shelter of that gulch, they would have been stark frozen corpses by morning.

For a blizzard arose. The snow had ceased to fall for a while, but now it began again. The cold had increased. A terrific wind arose. Even in the shelter of the gulch it was appalling. It roared and howled, tearing down the gully, thrashing the tops of the trees, making a veritable din of grisly, shrieking sounds. There was fuel in plenty, and they built a roaring fire. They knew how hard they must fight to keep from being frozen during that bitter night. The wind tore at their fire, snatched blazing embers and threw them about. The men built two fires and sat between them, their hats jammed down over their eyes, huddled against the terrible gale. The flying embers lighted on their clothes, their hats, their hands and faces.

There was no sleep at all for them that night. They fought the cold and the biting, flying embers. By dawn they were a pair of desperate and suffering men. Their hands and faces were blistered in numerous places, Hawke's thick Stetson had holes burned through it in several spots, there were countless holes in their clothes, even some in their shoes, all caused by those embers blown upon them by the raw wind. And still the wind roared, the snow flew. Drawn and haggard of face, grimed with smoke, soot and ashes, their eyes sunken and bloodshot, their stomachs nauseated by hunger, they considered their next move. They must climb that bluff. There was no other way. East and north lay the Bad Lands, west lay Lander, south over the bluff, promising haven and food, lay the ranches along the Sweetwater. As they stood looking at it they felt a sense of despair. It was so high, and they were so exhausted. But it had to be done.

There is little good in describing that terrible day. They tried to get up the bluff. But the snow was deep, thigh-deep, and the thin crust frozen over the top would not hold them. The going was extremely difficult, more so than either of them had imagined. During the night the busy wind had heaped and piled the drifts. They battled through the dry, impeding snow, breaking through the crust, floundering and falling, up again and on. But they were so weakened and the exertion was so great that they were little more than halfway to the rim of the bluff before the early twilight began to fall.

There was only one thing to do. They struggled back down into the gulch, built of branches the best shelter they could devise, ate all the rest of the rose pods, built a roaring fire, and prepared for another nightmare till dawn. *Four days without food,* save for the life-saving rose pods. The shelter helped, but again there was no sleep and the men were half crazed by the terrible ordeal. In the dawn they faced their last stand. This time they must go up the bluff or die.

Smoky was utterly hopeless. He said he could never make it, he was too near gone. Hawke laughed grimly. They would make it, or freeze. He told Smoky to buck up, he'd go ahead and break trail. So a second time they started up the bluff. The trail they had broken the day before aided their progress part of the way, but at that they went slowly. Every time they paused to rest it seemed they could not go on. Every time Hawke found it more difficult to get Smoky started again. Like two crazed animals they finally came to a stop, still a good way from the top. Smoky slumped onto the snow, lifting his grimy, drawn face, his breath coming in gasps. "Go on—make it to the top—if you can. I'm done. All in. It's the end of the trail—for me."

Hawke scowled, staring insanely at Smoky with

bloodshot eyes. Smoky sat with his back against the wall of the path, a wall of snow which had been made by their breaking through the crust as they advanced. Hawke argued desperately. They must go on. If they didn't make it now, they couldn't possibly do it later. Smoky was so nearly exhausted that no argument, promise or plea could arouse him to further effort. Hawke became frantic. If they could once get to the top of the bluff, all they had to do was go on and they would reach some ranch by the Sweetwater. He could make it, he was sure he could. But he couldn't leave Smoky behind. Neither could he aid him. He would need every ounce of his strength to get himself to the top.

He leaned over Smoky and drew his knife. He must have been a formidable sight, the drooping black mustache and black curls grimed with soot and ashes, the black eyes bloodshot and hard, half mad, the dark face drawn, blistered and smutted, set in an ugly threat. He brandished the knife.

"You'll go on!" his voice was hoarse and rasping. "You'll go on to the top or I'll cut your throat. And don't think I won't. I'll cut your throat before I'll leave you here to freeze. Get up!"

Smoky quailed. He fully believed that Hawke would do it. He stumbled to his feet, and Hawke continued to threaten him with the knife. The effort of driving Smoky on, the strain of making him believe the threat, partly took Hawke's mind off his own torturing desire to give up and drop in the snow. In a hazy, distorted nightmare, they battled on. They reached the top. It had taken them five hours. They sank in the snow to rest. Hawke's knife disappeared into his pocket. Neither of them said anything about it. Desperate as they were, ravaged and suffering, their brains were still working. They knew they dared not sit there long. They flogged themselves into action, and started on again—to come across the trail of a horse through the snow. Scattered along it were pieces of fresh beef. Someone had been stringing poisoned bait for wolves. For five hours or more they followed that trail, and a ranch came in sight. But it was after dark when they reached the ranch.

Those at the ranch knew they were fugitives, their terrible condition needed no explanation. But the rancher and his wife showed a humaneness that Hawke remembers to this day. "Be sure to say how good those people were to us," he cautioned me when we were gathering this data. "They, and every rancher we met, were damned white. They deserve to be remembered. They took us right in, there at that ranch on the Sweetwater. They gave us warm water and towels so we could wash up and get halfway clean again. The woman hustled around and got us a good hot supper. Five days without food, in forty below zero weather. And food cooked by a good woman cook. Did that supper taste good!" One can only faintly imagine what such treatment meant to those two.

It meant so much that today, long, long years after, Hawke grows quite vehement in praise of the Sweetwater people. While the men were eating their supper, they heard the rattle of a buckboard outside. Hawke was immediately disturbed for fear it was Sheriff Atkins. Smoky said he didn't care, if it was the devil and all his angels he wasn't going to leave his supper. But Hawke got up from the table and slipped outside, keeping to the cover of the shadows, and followed the buckboard to the barn. In the light of a lantern, carried by the driver as he prepared to put away his horses, Hawke saw that the man with the buckboard was Blondy. Blondy, whom Hawke had prosecuted in Lander for his row with Three-Fingered Jackson. But Blondy was human, genial and friendly; he had been acquitted. Hawke figured that the big blond gunman might not hold any resentment, and stepped toward him.

"Well I'll be damned!" Blondy stared, then chuckled. "So this is where you've got to, eh? You certainly have raised hell in Lander, old timer. Sheriff Atkins is right on your trail. You better travel fast tomorrow."

"I intend to," Hawke agreed mildly. "Where you headed for?"

"On my way from Lander to my ranch down at Buffalo." Blondy stepped a bit closer, and dropped his voice confidentially. "Keep away from the stage road, Hawke. Atkins is coming that way with a couple of deputies and a pack outfit. Tell you what you do. Go north, to the Rattlesnake Hills. Up there at the base of the hills there's a line camp. The punchers are good boys. They'll treat you right. I'll tell you how to get there."

Blondy was as good as his word. He gave them minute directions for reaching the line camp, and the next morning, rested and strengthened, Hawke and Smoky traveled on from the friendly ranch on the Sweetwater, following Blondy's directions and heading for the line camp at the base of the Rattlesnake Hills. The weather was better now, clear and cold, and no snow falling. They were still worn, their strength badly depleted, but they were certainly much better than they had been.

Blondy's directions had been accurate and detailed. The jail-breakers found the line camp without any trouble, and they found the punchers friendly. They were invited to stay as long as they liked. They stayed three days, resting and renewing their strength. At the ranch on the Sweetwater they had scrubbed away most of the ashes and grime from their hands and faces. Here in the line camp they finished the job of getting clean and shaved again. The third day, in the morning, one of the punchers glanced out a window and saw a rider approaching from the direction of the Sweetwater. He called Hawke's attention to the approaching horseman. It might be the sheriff. It might be a deputy. It might be anybody.

There was a rifle hanging on deerhorn supports over the fireplace. The puncher gave it to Hawke, and Hawke slipped out to the stable. There he kept watch, the rifle ready. But the horseman proved to be another puncher from a ranch below, and he had come for the express purpose of warning Hawke and Smoky that the sheriff was on the way. The puncher had learned from Blondy which way the fugitives had gone. The men at the line camp gave Hawke and Smoky all the cooked food they could carry, and the fugitives hurried on. They crossed over the range and went down a branch of the Dry Powder River. Hawke was eager to reach a small town which was ahead of them, on the Powder. But Smoky was determined to keep away from the settlement.

They spent two more nights in the open, and, their cooked food long gone, kept themselves from hunger by living on steak. Beefsteak, cut from the carcasses of cattle strung along the Dry Powder, cattle frozen to death in that grim winter. Hundreds of cattle perished in that particularly bitter season. The region between the Powder and the Black Hills was fairly well settled. At a ranch a little farther on, Smoky got a job feeding stock. Hawke proceeded down the Powder, alone. He never saw Smoky again.

For a long time that jail break from Lander was the subject of much conversation and speculation in the town and its surrounding territory. What Blondy and the line riders knew they kept to themselves. It remained a mystery, how the two men ever made their way alive through the wild country and bitter weather. No least trace of them was found. The few who had aided in their escape certainly would not betray them. They had done what the rustlers in Lander jail had branded as impossible. They had made good their escape.

Smoky was secure in a fine berth at the ranch where he had stopped, and Hawke went on to the settlement looking for a like opportunity, as he expressed it, "to hole in for a while and let the stink blow over." He was looking for a place where he could sink quietly into obscurity, live quietly through the rest of the winter and go on when spring came. He was looking for quiet! But what he found!

VI

Two days after leaving Smoky, Hawke reached the settlement. There were a few houses, a big general store and a stage station. Hawke approached the stage station, and found the stage tender out in the stable currying his horses. Hawke was a hard-looking specimen, ragged and unkempt, his face covered with a stubble of crinkly beard that had grown since he left the line camp. It wasn't surprising that the stage tender surveyed him with suspicion. Added to his appearance was the fact that he was afoot, and in that country a man didn't walk when there was a horse to be begged, borrowed or stolen. Hawke casually stated that he had come from the new oil camp over near the Dry Powder, that he didn't like it, and wondered if there was any place around there where a man could get a job.

The stage tender eyed him for a moment, then gestured toward the big general store, a short distance away, down and across the street. "See that jasper over there on the porch at the store? That's Link Woody. He's the only man around here that needs anybody to work for him, and he's always needin' somebody. You might go ask him."

There was something veiled in the man's voice

that caught Hawke's attention. It was largely the manner in which he said that Woody was always needing somebody. Hawke asked no questions, but very much on the alert he crossed to the store, introduced himself to Woody under the first handy alias he could call to mind, and asked if Woody could give him a job.

He didn't like Woody's looks at all. He fancied that one look at Woody quite explained why the man was "always needin' somebody." He was a big fellow, several inches taller than Hawke, with a coarse, dark face. The general tone of his complexion and the peculiar bloated look about him evidenced the fact that he was a very heavy drinker and had been for years. His eyes were penetrating yet evasive, the expression of his face decidedly lowering and ill-tempered. The appearance of the man did not give Hawke pause. He must get into hiding quickly, and have a chance to sleep and eat regularly, lest the ravages of the escape from Lander permanently impair his health. If Woody was the only man in the territory who needed help, he would not hesitate to work for Woody. Because Woody's personality was offensive to him was no reason for his recuperating any the less efficiently on Woody's ranch.

Woody looked him over carefully, and replied that he could certainly use another man. He was building a new stable and corrals at his ranch, the

W Bar S, and he needed more help in cutting and hauling logs and poles. So Hawke was hired by Link Woody within fifteen minutes after he had entered the settlement, and departed from the settlement to his place of temporary retirement, Woody's W Bar S ranch. Link Woody, by the way, is the man's name, *was* the man's name. He has been dead for many years. He and Hawke drove to the ranch in an old buckboard. Woody admitted frankly that he could not afford to pay any wages, that all Hawke could expect in return for his labor was a good place to sleep and plenty of food to eat, and Hawke began to understand why Link Woody was always needing somebody. He also began to understand the dry under-current that had been in the stage tender's voice when the man referred him to Woody.

Hawke concerned himself little with the fact that he would be working solely for lodging and food. Even that was to his advantage. If Woody was that hard up, the chances were excellent that his ranch would be left pretty well alone. Doubtless a very good place of retirement indeed. When they arrived at the ranch, Hawke came into contact with the surprising shifting of life's currents. He found at the W Bar S a small person-nel or rough-looking characters, and he found Joe Towers. Towers also had come there to remain in concealment for a while, though he did not say just what he had been doing to make concealment advisable and desirable. Neither did Hawke. With the months between a closed issue, the two greeted each other as if they had parted but the day before, and joined forces again. Joe had already been there several days, nearly two weeks to be exact.

After the evening meal, he and Hawke withdrew to the barn to talk things over confidentially. "What kind of an outfit is this, anyway?" Hawke asked. "I didn't like Woody's looks from the start, but he was a kind of last resort. Any old port in a storm, you know. A man who isn't craving publicity can't be over-finical when it comes to picking a spot for cover. The more I see of the place the less I like it. What are they, rustlers?"

"Name 'em and you can have 'em," Towers grinned. "I don't believe they're rustlers. I guess I have no kick coming. They work you hard but they feed you good. I thought from the way you looked at that slim fellow that you must have seen him before. I mean the fellow who calls himself Streeter. Seen him somewhere?"

"Maybe I have—in jail. Again, maybe I haven't. He answers the description of Slim Brennan, who used to belong to the Butch McLaughlin gang of road agents. Same hard blue eyes, same thin lips, same long chin with a scar. But I guess there isn't much to choose between Streeter and Woody. Tough hombres, both of them."

Towers agreed with him, without reservation. Neither Hawke nor Towers had any fancy for the

W Bar S, but it would take something infinitely more drastic than present conditions to alter their determination to remain there until better weather came. Before many days had passed, Hawke found something else to attract his interest at the ranch. Woody had a step-daughter, a young girl about eighteen or nineteen years of age. He also had a son, the girl's half brother. The girl's name was Alma Barnes and the boy's name was Terry. He was several years younger than his half sister. Both boy and girl were of finer caliber than Link Woody, were sadly out of place on the dubious spread of the W Bar S.

It was characteristic of Hawke that he decided to make certain that the boy and the girl were not held there by force, and if they were, not to leave the ranch until he had seen them safely away from there to whatever place they wished to reach. It didn't take him long to acquire a comprehensive survey of the situation. Alma Barnes was an uncommonly pretty girl, and the man who called himself Streeter made no attempt to disguise his awareness of that fact. The girl was uncomfortable and unhappy, and not a little afraid. But she was fond of the little boy, and her instinct, maternal and protective, wouldn't allow her to go from the ranch and leave the child unguarded in that atmosphere. Terry was Woody's son, and she couldn't very well take him away. Too, she had no other place to go. So she remained at the W Bar S, silently enduring an uncomfortable situation and hoping that something would happen to release her and the boy. Streeter was the man she seemed to fear most. He was distinctly the killer type. This was the situation Hawke had fathomed in a few days. He saw no way in which he could change matters, at least for the time being. He devoted his attention to regaining his strength, eating well and sleeping better.

He and Joe had been there several weeks and Hawke was quite himself again, when the two of them were sitting in front of the bunkhouse one early evening, watching Streeter and Woody work on a two-year-old colt in the corral. Alma Barnes came around the bunkhouse and stopped close to them. She glanced quickly about, to assure herself that no one else was within hearing distance, then spoke to Hawke in lowered tones.

You men had better go tonight. My step-father and Streeter are planning to get rid of you. I heard them."

"Yes?" Hawke glanced at Woody and Streeter, then turned his gaze on the girl. "What's the idea?"

A bitter and scornful expression crossed the girl's face. "They've no further use for you. Most of the hard work is done. I've no compunction about telling you, you've both been very nice to Terry and me, and the main trouble is that you'll be in their way when they begin to rustle stock. I didn't hear them say what they intended doing with you, but I did hear them mention some man they expected from over Inyan Kara way. If you two are hiding from the authorities, it's none of my business, but you had better go while there's time." And the girl was gone before either of the men could make any reply.

Hawke and Towers decided that it might be well for them to move on after dark. As it was growing dusk the man expected by Woody rode up to the corral. He was a lanky, stoop-shouldered man, elderly, perhaps fifty or more. He wore the garb of a cowpuncher, and two six-shooters on his single belt. Streeter and Woody met him at the corral, the three talked there for a few moments, then walked to the bunkhouse, where Streeter remained. Woody and the elder man went on to the house.

Hawke and Towers had as yet found no opportunity to slip quietly away. They said nothing to Streeter when he came in the bunkhouse, they knew by his actions that he was there to watch them. About an hour later Woody and the elder man came to the bunkhouse. As they entered the door, Streeter, as though their entrance were a signal, drew his guns and covered Hawke and Towers. They two had been expecting something of the kind, said nothing and made no resistance when Woody proceeded to bind their wrists behind their backs.

A short while afterward, Woody went out and brought up three horses, saddled and ready to ride, one each for Hawke and Towers and one for Streeter. Streeter ordered them onto the horses, helped them into their saddles and then got onto the back of his own mount. Woody and the other man went to the corral, and came back presently mounted. At Woody's orders, the five set out across the plain toward the northeast.

Hawke was alert to every move, wondering mightily. Both he and Joe had been supplied with a Henry rifle, the guns being thrust into the boots on the saddles. Hawke guessed shrewdly that both of these guns were empty. Nothing of their destination was said for some time, and they rode till dawn. They stopped for breakfast in a secluded cove near the Powder. The horses were turned out to graze. It was there that Woody baldly explained to them what they were going to do. They were riding toward an isolated store building. The owner of the building lived back of his store and usually had a good deal of money there. They were going to hold up the store. Hawke and Towers were to hold up the store, and the elder man would be right behind them. He admitted frankly, with a dry grin, that the guns carried by Hawke and Towers would be empty. The other man's gun would not be empty.

To Woody's surprise, Hawke made no least objection; which would have made Woody suspicious had he known with what kind of man he was dealing. Hawke was planning swiftly. He could see farther than Woody gave him credit for being able to see. He and Joe would be forced to hold up the store keeper, with empty guns and without masks. The elder man would wear a mask, also carry a loaded gun. After the robbery, Hawke and Towers would be turned loose, while Woody and the others departed hastily with the loot. If Hawke and Joe had heard anything at the W Bar S which might be against Woody and Streeter, they would be effectually quieted. They would be forced to leave the country as swiftly as possible, or they would be arrested and jailed for the robbery of the store.

Hawke smiled to himself. Woody had over-reached. His own pure cussedness would play into the hands of Hawke and Joe. Hawke agreed amiably to the robbery of the store, which put Woody in a more pleasant mood.

They remained in the cove until dinner time, got another meal and moved on, and Hawke noted that they were very careful to avoid the few ranches they passed. Without seeing anyone, and without being seen, they reached the vicinity of the isolated store as the day waned. They left the horses on a small flat, some distance from the store, well hidden in the plum trees and willows growing there. Here they ate another meal, cold, since they did not wish to build a fire so near the store, and waited for darkness. They continued to wait until the last customer had visited and left the store, and they could see the keeper inside, moving about, preparatory to closing up for the night. The elder man tied a bandana across his face, covered Towers and Hawke and ordered them to proceed with the business at hand.

The thing was surprisingly easy. There were two men in the store; the other came in from a back room as the holdups entered the front door. Both the men were proprietors, it developed, and neither of them made any resistance. In short time, Towers, Hawke and the elder man backed out with their loot, which consisted of all the money they had found in the safe, tobacco, cartridges, foodstuffs and several bottles of whiskey.

The elder man forced his two prisoners, Hawke and Joe, to hurry across to the flat where Woody and Streeter waited with the horses. There they told Hawke and Joe to ride, and keep going. The horses were mere nags, the rifles were empty, and Joe presently voiced his curiosity at Hawke's easy acquiescence in the whole deal. Hawke smiled.

"You wait and see. Those three are going for the ranch as fast as they can move. The store keeper will hunt up an officer and a posse to come after us. That's all I'm waitin' for. Just let 'em come!"

Joe grinned in sudden enlightenment. If there

was one thing a robber wouldn't do, it was ride straight back to meet the posse trailing him. Hawke was planning shrewdly. He and Joe paused a little way from the store, within easy hearing distance, and slept till daylight. With the first light they were up, waiting and listening. They had no difficulty in ascertaining the presence of the posse a few hours later. The men were talking excitedly when they stopped at the store, and Hawke and Joe promptly rode to meet them. The hastily gathered posse consisted of one of the store keepers, six men from different ranches, and a deputy sheriff, in charge. The store keeper cried out in excitement as Hawke and Towers rode into sight, exclaiming that those were the men who had robbed the store.

"Quite right," Hawke assured him. "We're from the W Bar S ranch. My statement will be borne out by the brands on our horses. We held you up, with empty guns, because a man with a loaded gun was behind us." Rapidly and succinctly, Hawke detailed the entire episode, and invited the officer to examine the guns in their saddle boots and see for himself that they were empty.

The deputy sheriff nodded slowly, and turned to the store keeper. "That explains why these two were not masked. Well," he addressed Hawke, "anyone with half an eye can see that you boys are honest. Are you willing to go with us to run down that gang?"

Hawke surveyed him with a mild smile. "Why do you think we waited around here for you? We could have kept going, you know. If you'll supply us with some shells, I'll be delighted to lead the attack."

The posse men rode on, not aimlessly now, as they would ride in a blind chase, but hard on a straight course, led by Hawke and Joe. They lost as little time as possible in stopping to rest and eat. Hawke explained to the officer the general layout of the ranch. He explained also that there were loopholes in the walls of the house. That one of the outfit was always on watch with a long-range rifle. The approach to the ranch would have to be made after dark and with caution. The girl and the boy would have to be gotten away from there before the posse could pour in a hail of lead to subdue and overcome Woody's small but ugly crew.

It was well after dusk when they came within sight of the ranch, and halted on a ridge to the west to gaze down at the dim blot of shadow made by the buildings in the swiftly fading light. The officer frowned and remarked that it wasn't going to be easy. The buildings stood in the clear, two hundred yards at least from any cover. Hawke suggested that the posse make no attempt to get within shooting distance until he had brought the girl and boy from the house, which he would do as soon as it was quite dark and he saw the lights go on in the house. The officer protested that it was a suicidal thing to do, with Woody and Streeter both killers and desperate men. Before Hawke could reply, one of the posse men, a puncher from a ranch below the store, offered a dry remark.

"I reckon Hawke Travis can take care of himself, sheriff, if half of what I heard back in Idaho was true."

Hawke stiffened in his saddle, literally holding his breath. "What the hell did you hear about me, and who told you I was Hawke Travis?"

The man laughed, an abrupt laugh that died in an amused chuckle. "Don't fly off the handle, Travis. I heard enough to know when to mind my own business concerning you, and to know that if anybody can walk down into that hornet's nest and come back with a whole hide, you're it."

Hawke relaxed. "You don't want to believe all you hear," he returned, and gave his attention to the deputy sheriff. All he wanted, he said, was a Colt. The man from Idaho spurred up his horse, halted alongside Hawke and offered him one of the two guns he carried. In the waning light the two men looked each other squarely in the eye, and Hawke laughed in understanding as he accepted the gun.

No one had anything more to say. Hawke thrust the Colt inside the waistband of his trousers, slipped out of the saddle and started down the hill toward the ranch, with a parting suggestion that the men leave their horses in the grove below the corral. He made no attempt to conceal his movements. It was so dark now that it would be impossible for anyone to see him from the house until he was much closer. He reached the foot of the hill and paused about three hundred yards from the house. He had crossed the plains with bulls and wagon, he had fought the Indians, and he had learned about fighting from them. He resorted now to an Indian trick. He broke off a large piece of sage-brush. Into its branches close about the main stem he stuffed handfuls of dried grass. Then flat on his belly he crawled slowly toward the house, hidden behind the sage-brush which he held in his hand before his face.

So slowly did he move, so completely was he hidden, that it would have taken a sharp eye indeed to detect the fact that that especial clump of sage was moving. He came within a hundred yards of the house and paused to listen. Inside the building, the men were talking loudly, laughing and singing snatches of ribald songs. Evidently they were making very merry with the whiskey they had taken from the store. He resumed his snail-like progress toward the house, reached it, got cautiously to his feet, and peered through the window which he knew opened into the girl's room.

The door between her room and the living room

was closed. She was standing by the door, listening to the sounds from the other room. The boy was lying on the bed, watching her. Both of them were patently excited and frightened. Hawke tapped on the window pane with the barrel of his Colt. The boy sprang up on the bed, and the girl whirled to face the window, her eyes widening in fright. Then she recognized Hawke's face, and hurried to the window.

"You must get out of here at once," Hawke spoke lowly, through the small space where a corner of the pane had been broken out. "The place is surrounded by a posse, ready to open fire the moment I have you and the boy safely away."

The girl shivered. "But I can't open the window, Mr. Travis. It's nailed shut."

Hawke gestured with his head toward the door opening into the other room. "Who's in there?"

"All of them. Streeter and Woody, and that fellow from Inyan Kara. And they're all drunk. They've been talking horribly, and making all kinds of terrible threats. Terry and I were frightened to death. I don't dare try to go through that room, and I can't open the window. You'd better tell your posse to go ahead and fire. Terry and I will hide the best we can, under the bed or some place, where we won't be likely to get hit. But tell them to act quickly, and not let Woody and Streeter get away. They're terrible men. I—I heard them talking about the robbery."

Travis frowned and shook his head. "No. You're coming out of there. You and the boy stand right here by the window. I'll break out the pane, and it won't take me long to do it. I'll lift you and the boy through, and you run as fast as you can go till you reach the posse; go in a straight line from the front door. You'll be in no danger. None of the posse will fire until he hears my signal. Get ready."

Badly frightened, but decidedly courageous, the girl caught the boy off the bed and drew him with her against the wall close to the window, holding over them both a blanket she had snatched up from the bed, to prevent the breaking glass from flying in their faces.

It was an amazingly daring thing to do, with three drunken men in the next room, certain to hear the sound of the breaking glass. Speed was the necessary thing, and Hawke had it. He crashed the glass out of the window with several lightning swift blows, and reached for the boy: as he drew the child out the window, set him on the ground and reached for the girl, he heard Woody inquire with a curse what was the noise in the girl's room. There came a scuffle of feet and the scrape of chairs as the men rose from their carousal and started for the door to the girl's room. Before any of them reached that door, the girl was on the ground outside, had gripped the child's hand and started with him, running at top speed, to join the posse. Streeter flung the door open, but Hawke had faded out of sight, and all Streeter saw was an empty room and a broken window.

Hawke darted around the house, knowing that the attention of all three temporarily would be centered on that empty room, and paused for a moment by the door opening into the living room. The signal to the posse was to be a single shot from his revolver. But there was a signal for which he too waited, the low whistle from Joe Towers that was to apprise him of the fact that the girl and the boy had reached the posse in safety. It seemed a long minute that he waited by the door, hearing within the excited and angry comments of Streeter and Woody. Then the low whistle drifted across the clearing. The girl and the boy were safe.

Hawke shoved open the plank door of the house, and leaped inside the room, his gun leveled, snapping at the men an order to throw up their hands. All three of them obeyed the command, and stood staring at him as if they could not believe their eyes. They seemed dumbfounded by his sheer daring. Not a one of them spoke, and Woody shook his head like a man coming out of a daze. Hawke was not standing erect, but in a half crouch, ready to leap or fire at the first necessity for it.

He heard no step behind him. He had no idea there was anyone else on the ranch, but there was a fourth man, come in that night to join the fellow from Inyan Kara. This man had heard the breaking glass, and had come running to the house from the bunkhouse. He stepped up behind Hawke and jammed the muzzle of his Colt against Hawke's shoulder.

"Drop it!" he snapped.

In the next instant he was a very much surprised man. Hawke knew that if he submitted to capture now he had no more chance to get out of there alive than, in his own words, a snowball in hell. He went over, forward, aided by that preparatory crouch he had assumed. His head went down toward his feet. Doubled up like a ball, he threw himself backward, rolling, hurling his body at the feet of the man who had thrust a gun against his back. As he ducked, he snapped a shot at Link Woody, and Link slumped, badly wounded. The man behind Hawke had had his finger on the trigger ready to fire. He did fire, as Hawke doubled, but the shot went harmlessly over Hawke's back; the next instant Hawke struck his feet like a missile from a catapult and the man went sprawling on his face, while Hawke rolled out into the yard and leaped to his feet, dodging aside. Both Streeter and the other man opened fire on him, but no one hit him.

The posse, hearing the firing, closed in on a run, hurling a volley of bullets at the house. Realizing that they were trapped, Streeter and the other men inside the house closed the door, sprang to barricading it and the windows. The posse rushed up to the house, close enough to meet Hawke, who came running toward them. Hawke explained that he had winged Woody, and that doubtless the others would barricade themselves in and return a dangerous fire.

"Well, we'll give 'em a chance to surrender peaceably," the deputy sheriff returned. He raised his voice in a shout: "Hi, you fellows in there. Come out with your hands up. I've got the house surrounded. A jackrabbit couldn't get by us. Deputy sheriff and posse. Better come out without any nonsense."

The answer he received was a blaze of fire from a couple of the loopholes Hawke had described and a sardonic and scornful laugh from Streeter. The deputy remarked that it was rather useless to besiege the building in that fashion. The men inside could fire with telling effect, enough to keep them at a distance, and might very conceivably wound or kill some of the posse. Hawke shrugged. His dynamite temper was up. Making no reply to the deputy, he turned back to the house, saying in an undertone, "Come on, Joe." He broke into a run, and not until he reached the house did he realize that there were two men at his heels. The puncher from Idaho had joined Joe. Hawke came to a halt by the broken window in the room that had been occupied by the girl.

"They're all in the other room," Hawke explained swiftly. "They'll have everything barricaded by this time. They won't be looking for anybody to come in this way. We're going to get them. Joe, you set that back wall afire, then follow me."

As Hawke climbed through the window, he heard Joe and the man from Idaho scratching matches. It would be a simple matter to set fire to the house there. A small lean-to was built against that wall. The whole structure was as dry as tinder. As a matter of fact, Joe and the man from Idaho had flames leaping up the wall within five minutes. But within that five minutes several things had happened. Hawke was inside the girl's room. He stepped to the door opening between it and the living room. He could hear the men talking and cursing in the next room. Evidently they had no fear that the posse would come very close to the house. And as evidently they had no least intention of surrendering.

Hawke waited tensely, wanting the fire to gain some headway. It was gaining fast enough. Joe and the man from Idaho had built it and fed it with heaps of the dry pitch wood in the lean-to. Already the posse saw the blaze, and stood watching to see what Hawke and the other two men intended. When Hawke heard the crackle of the flames, and saw through the broken window the rising light of the fire, he decided it was time to act.

He looked about for a suitable battering instrument. The only thing available was a straight-backed chair with a heavy wooden bottom. Hawke thrust his gun into his waistband, snatched up the chair and brought it against the door with all his strength. He aimed the blow at the exact spot where the latch was set in the door. The heavy blow broke the latch and the door moved against the inadequate barricade on the other side. Before the men in the other room could have more than turned a startled glance, Hawke rained several other blows on the door, breaking it loose from its leather hinges and sending it down. Woody was too badly wounded to give battle. But the man from Inyan Kara whirled, his face savage with rage, and fired at Hawke. The heavy slug missed Hawke's head and embedded itself in the bottom of the chair Hawke had just swung upward.

Now the other Inyan Kara man, who had attempted to hold Hawke up in the doorway, turned from his post and came toward Hawke, jerking up his gun to fire. Hawke hurled the chair at him, struck him squarely in the stomach with it, and knocked the fellow to his back. The man's weapon went skittering across the floor. By that time, Streeter had opened fire on Hawke. And in a split second more, Hawke had whipped out his own gun and was making good use of it. Streeter went down under Hawke's second bullet. But so, also, did Hawke go down. Streeter had got him through the left shoulder. As Hawke sank to the floor, Joe Towers and the man from Idaho came sprawling in through the window, darted around the bed to reach Hawke and opened fire on the two men remaining in the living room, the only two left of Woody's small but vicious outfit capable of putting up a fight. Woody was almost unconscious, Streeter was dead. As Joe and the man from Idaho, guns spitting, halted above Hawke's prone figure, the deputy sheriff and others of the posse began pounding on the front door.

It was too hot for the two men from Inyan Kara, and they were men from a desperate band of outlaws. But an armed posse was besieging one door, two furious punchers were shooting through another door. And smoke was pouring in all along the back wall, flames were licking through a loophole in one place. The two men had had enough. They threw down their guns and held up their hands. The man from Idaho kept them covered, while Joe opened the front door and let the posse in. It remained only to get everybody out of the doomed house.

Results of that battle sum quickly. Joe wounded one of the Inyan Kara men, not a dangerous wound but a painful one. Streeter was not the outlaw Hawke had suspected him to be, but he was another equally as bad. Woody lived to stand trial for robbing the store. The house burned to the ground, consumed to the last board along with everything the men had stolen from the store, except the money. That was hidden in the bunkhouse, and the store keeper got it back.

This hole in the shoulder was Hawke's first serious wound. He lost a great quantity of blood, and felt very weak and useless when Joe and the man from Idaho carried him out to the bunkhouse. As the posse was ready to leave with the prisoners, the deputy sheriff offered to put Hawke up at his house till he was thoroughly recovered from his wound. The store keeper made the same offer. Hawke refused both. There was sufficient food in Woody's cook house and root cellar. He preferred to stay there in the bunkhouse until his wound was healed, with Joe to wait on him. The officer protested. He ought to see a doctor. Hawke only laughed. It didn't amount to a whoop in hell, he assured the other man.

The officer ceased arguing, took his prisoners and his posse and went away. Undisturbed, Hawke and Joe Towers stayed there alone in the bunkhouse at the W Bar S till the food gave out. By that time, Hawke was completely recovered from his wound, the weather was warming to spring, and Hawke and Joe Towers parted again. Hawke might have died there in that bunkhouse, blood poison might have set into the wound. But he doggedly stayed there and took care of himself with Joe's help, fearing that any kind of publicity concerning him might reach the sheriff at Lander.

He never knew what became of Alma Barnes and the boy, but there were kindly people in the settlement to take them in. At least she was freed from Woody, who was sent to the penitentiary, and who died there. Joe Towers was eager to go farther west, but Hawke did not want to go that way. They parted, dividing between them what was left of the food. That was the last time Hawke ever saw Joe Towers.

As Hawke rode away, alone and on the trail again, he had come to a pass of serious thought. He had killed several men, yet in spite of the fact that the dead men had richly deserved killing, the thought of it made Hawke a little sick. What, he asked himself, was life getting him? He had taken great pains to acquire deadly skill with his Colt forty-four, and what had that got him? A reputation as a gunman with uncanny ability. He shifted in the saddle uneasily, as he thought of it. The reputation was certain to precede him or follow him, wherever he went, as it had followed him from Idaho. He would be forced to kill again, and yet again, or would be killed by some other gunman. He could see no future for the man who persisted in being a law unto himself. All the forces of the universe, the forces that worked for good at least, were against him.

The best thing he could do was to leave his

lawlessness behind, get a job, make a useful citizen of himself and settle down. He rode with that thought in mind. He stopped at ranches here and there along the Belle Fourche and found only open welcome. A short time later he reached Deadwood, hungry and weary and broke. He had been in Deadwood before. He found there a saloon keeper he had known in the past. The saloon keeper supplied him with enough money to rent a room and buy a few meals. He spent a few months in Deadwood, doing odd jobs and playing poker when no work was to be had. When the spring was well open he went to work in a brickyard and accumulated a fair-sized stake. Then his feet began to itch again.

Do I wish I could say that Hawke now "went straight," and made a spectacular comeback to the ways of law and order? I don't know. He was a character of the Old West. He was beginning to realize that something was wrong somewhere, either with himself or with social conditions. What it was he didn't know. He must have been born to wander, he couldn't seem to stay for any length of time in any one place. Had his temper, his daring or his very human vanity been less, it might be a different story to grow here as I write. But this is a human document, the colorful and swiftly moving story of a man's life. I can't imagine him as anything so inconsistent as the impeccable heroes one finds in some fiction.

Whatever one might wish to record, the fact is that the money Hawke now accumulated had been won at poker as much as it had been earned in the brickyard.

A goodly quantity of it had been won from soldiers stationed at Fort Meade, and from citizens working at the post. Hawke had acquired a sharp skill from a poker shark in Lander. He admits, with a chuckle and a spark in his eyes, that the ease with which he had been winning, at the post, had inflated his ego disgracefully. He thought he was a "real sport." The work at the brickyard was hard. Why continue it when he could make more money playing poker? Hawke couldn't see any sense in that. He had heard that there were big games running in Yankton, and he decided to go over there and take a hand, with the idea of winning some real money.

He found the big games easily enough, and after the second play—he was broke. He was angered and humiliated. His pride was pricked. He had thought he was a first-class card shark. Yet these gamblers in Yankton had stripped him. He knew they were crooked, but he had no least idea how they had gone about it to break him so easily and quickly. Worse than the loss of the money, worse than the blow to his vanity, was the jeering remark with which one of the gamblers taunted him:

"Better learn some new graft before you set in with professionals. Thumbnail marks is old stuff."

The remark was meant only for a sarcastic thrust, but Hawke chose to see in it very good advice. In the stud games at the post, where there were no professional gamblers, thumbnail marks had served admirably, but they appeared to be a puerile device in the presence of genuinely sophisticated players. Early the next morning, Hawke was on the way to Sioux City. He had ridden a horse from the W Bar S, but he had long since sold it. He was broke, and could not ride the train. He walked. His intention was to take the first temporary job that offered itself. But this was a bad time of the year to find any work. He walked all day, down the road between orchards and fields, but that got tiresome. He decided to steal a horse and sell it in Sioux City. Just before nightfall, in a big pasture to the left of the road, he spied a big bay. The horse was young, very finely built, and was grazing among several other animals.

Hawke was hungry. He had had nothing to eat all day. He could ride to a ranch, as a drifting cowpuncher, and eat with the rest of the boys. But he couldn't, afoot and looking like a tramp, step up to the back door of a farm house and beg for "a handout." That quirk of stubborn pride again. He could steal a horse and ride for Sioux City, but he couldn't beg a meal of some farmer's wife. He determined to take this horse. But he felt very lean about the middle. Down the road a short distance was a big barn. It was meal time, all the men would be in the chuck house or the farm house. Hawke hurried on to the barn, approached it cautiously, and halted as he heard a supper bell ring at the house. Several men walked out of the barn and from adjoining cow sheds and departed toward the kitchen. Hawke slipped into the barn, picked up a pail he found in a stall, and proceeded to milk one of the cows. Several work horses were in their stalls, and numerous pieces of harness were about. Hawke departed with nearly a gallon of milk in the pail, and took refuge in a grove of timber near the road.

He remained there till ten o'clock at night, or something near that hour. He drank the whole gallon of milk. When the lights were all out at the house, he returned to the barn, put the pail back where he had got it, and walked off with the best saddle and bridle he could find. The bay horse was gentle. Hawke had no trouble in catching him, and a very short time later Hawke Travis was continuing his journey, in the saddle. He rode all night, and at dawn was within a mile of Sioux City. He concealed himself in a patch of timber, rested for a couple of hours and let the horse graze. Then he rode boldly down the road and stopped at the first livery stable he reached. He asked the proprietor if there was a horse buyer around.

"I'm a stranger here," he explained blandly.

"Just pulled in from Winnisheik County. My camp's a mile or two up the river. But I need a little money, so I thought I'd sell this bay."

The liveryman eyed both Hawke and the horse before he replied, "How much you want for him?" The query was oddly blunt, and Hawke's mind leaped to the conclusion that the man probably knew the horse. He did. He told Hawke his partner did all the buying, and he'd have to call him to see the animal. He stepped into the stable, and Hawke saw him stop and speak, in a low and excited manner, to another man. That was enough for Hawke.

He thumped his heels against the horse and went galloping down the street. At the first side street he turned toward the river. There on the bank he found a skiff. It was leaky, and it lacked oars, but Hawke leaped off the horse and hurried to the little boat. He unmoored it, sprang into it, pulled off a thwart and began to paddle across the muddy stream, using the thwart as an oar. Before he had gone fifty yards, the boat swamped under him. As he sank in the water, the livery man and a policeman came racing down the bank. Both of them began firing at Hawke. He was entirely submerged, save for his nose and forehead, he was holding one hand on the edge of the sunken boat and was paddling with the other hand.

The policeman and the livery man ceased firing and hurriedly got into a boat to follow him. They were within a hundred yards of him when he reached the shore, or rather when he reached a sand bar, and he darted out of the water into the willow trees growing on the sand bar. His pursuers emptied both guns at him. He heard the bullets whine around him and whip through the willow trees. But they never touched him.

He made his way into a deep gully. It was so choked with brush and vines that it was a very good hiding place. Hawke burrowed into the grass and weeds, and stayed there till dark. Under the cover of night he followed the gully to its head, and found a road running north and south. He went along the road till he came to another farm. Here he got a few ears of corn and some potatoes out of the field adjoining the road. He walked on for a couple of hours till he reached a timbered bottom along a small stream, and he was very thankful indeed that he made it a habit to carry a waterproof match box. He built a fire, roasted his corn and potatoes, dried his clothes thoroughly and got a few hours' sleep. By daylight he was again on the road, going south.

Somewhere around nine o'clock he came to a small tract of land, some twenty acres. The land was owned by a widow, and she was out in her small field putting up her hay. Amused and curious, Hawke paused to watch her for a moment. She saw him, stopped her work, leaned on the fork she had been using, and shouted at him, "Hey there! Looking for a job?"

"Sure thing!" Hawke called back, vaulted the rail fence and walked over to her. "Looking for one, but praying I won't find it."

The woman surveyed him with skeptical eyes. "That's the way with most of the tramps that come along this road. Ain't worth their salt. Eat all I'll give them, accept a night's lodging, then run out on me without doing a lick of work. You happen to know anything about haying?"

Hawke bowed, a mocking smile on his face. "Lady, I know *all* about it. Too much for my own good. I suppose that you want first to cock this that you have raked into windrows?"

The woman's gaze intensified, the skepticism in her eyes was mingled with puzzlement. "Say, what have you been up to? You don't talk or act like a bum, but you've been up to something. What makes your clothes so wrinkled that way?" Hawke grinned and said that he had got drunk and fallen in the river. The woman emitted a very unladylike snort of scorn. "You're a liar by the watch. But I don't care what you've been doing. I've got to have help with this hay."

Hawke sighed. "Seems like I'm always meeting somebody who has to have help with his hay."

"You been to breakfast yet?"

Hawke frowned in mock meditation. "Let's see. I believe I did have a bite of something or other two or three days ago. But don't put your-self out. I can stand it till noon."

"Don't talk to me. Come to the house and get something to eat, then you can go to work on the hay."

So Hawke got himself another job. He stayed there nearly a month. The woman was a good cook, good-natured and companionable. But, to Hawke's discomfort, she was in the market for another husband. Hawke had seen women look at him that way before, and he thought he had better move on. The woman was of the primitive kind. What she wanted she took, if possible, and did so without regard for the rules of ethics or morality. Hawke drew part of his wages on the pretext of buying some things he needed, and set off for town. But he didn't come back. He kept going south, and then the trail that lured his wandering feet turned, twisted and turned again.

Early the next spring he was back in the Rocky Mountains, located in a tie camp ten thousand feet above the sea level. During that winter, after he had left the widow's place, Hawke had married, had married a young girl of eighteen. But one only glimpses this chapter of his life; out of respect for penetralia in the abstract, and for that of Hawke and his wife in particular, one touches only the surface here. For her sake Hawke was resolved to be done with lawlessness, which was why he was in a tie camp cutting ties. It was harder work than he had ever done before. The red spruce in demand by the railroad company grew at a high altitude, and the timber trees among which Hawke was working spread over a steep mountain side. Hiatus.

Then the tie camp closed down and Hawke decided to have a ranch of his own. He filed on eighty acres of Government land. The tract lay at the western edge of a valley, a small but beautiful valley, in the very heart of the Colorado Rockies. The tract had been passed by, was unattractive to other homesteaders. It had been considered, by others who had viewed it, as worthless for anything save grazing. There was a good growth of timber on it, piñon and pines. Also on the tract there was a small cove, comprising about four acres and almost barren of timber. But all over the cove, sage-brush was growing, man high.

Hawke knew something of such land, land that could produce such giant sage. He had seen it in Idaho, Wyoming and Utah. It was fertile ground. It would produce enormous crops with the aid of water. South of the cove reared a bluff. Out of the bluff several springs spilled small, steady streams. The water from the springs could be run into a small storage reservoir, and the water used to irrigate the cove. There for a time, Hawke worked with all his energy. His place became known as the Ranch in the Cove. It was so called ever afterward. Now there came a shift in events, not to be recorded here. This chronicle is interested only in the results of those events.

The results are these: the girl Hawke had married was gone, and a child with her. Hawke was left alone on the ranch, where he had seen some happy days. He had a little surplus money, and nothing for which to use it. He was unbearably lonely. He took his money and sought company in town. Poker games were running, banking games were flourishing. A man with a hot head and a bruised heart could forget his loneliness. The town was a lively place, head-quarters for miners and ranchers from a wide radius. Quantities of money were in sight, the town was wide open, and the gamblers were making heyday.

One of the game keepers invited Hawke to sit in. Hawke accepted the invitation. He quit winner. But he was wise enough now to know that his winnings were due more to luck than to his superior ability as a poker player. He had tried to leave the lawlessness behind, but he had been embittered by events that discounted his endeavor to succeed at another kind of life. He remembered the jeering gambler in Yankton, and grimly determined to become a real professional. They'd have no chance to strip him and laugh at him again. It was too sickeningly lonely at the ranch. He tried to go back to it, but gradually stopped doing anything there save the merest chores. Every night he was back at the games. The result was inevitable.

He threw himself into gambling with the determination to learn everything about it there was to know. Since he had intelligence of a high order and used it, he very rapidly acquired the knowledge and skill he desired. Before long they at the gambling house realized that Hawke was a man with whom it was wiser for them to join forces, much wiser than it was for them to pit their skill against his. Within two months from the time Hawke first entered the gambling house, determined to learn the tricks of the trade, he was a full-fledged gambler and a partner in the business. Hawke took charge of the crap game, while his partner ran the roulette wheel. For some reason the play was heavier at the wheel than it was at the crap game, very much heavier. Hawke's partner began to take advantage of the fact.

He began to knock down a good percentage of the winnings. For a while Hawke merely watched and said nothing. After thinking the matter over, he decided merely to quit the man, and not make any trouble. None the loser, and very much wiser, he looked about for another partner. There was nothing to be found in this town, so he departed for Cripple Creek. The great gold camp was producing large quantities of high-grade ore, and gambling was ripe in Cripple Creek. Hawke had confidential information concerning conditions there. Much of the rich ore mined in the gold camp, a large quantity of the very richest ore, in fact, never reached the ore houses "on top," and never helped to augment the dividends of the mine owners.

It was stolen by miners, carried off in their pockets and in numerous ways, and sold to crooked assayers who had established offices in various places about the district. This business of "glomming" rich ore and making money on the side was very easily accomplished. Easy come, easy go. Most of the glommers lost it about as fast as they made it, lost it in the gambling houses. Hawke thought Cripple Creek certainly looked like easy picking.

He looked about for a day or two, striving to locate an opening. He found it, in a saloon on Second Street near the heart of the red-light district. The saloon, dive, joint—or whatever you want to call it—was one of the toughest in Cripple Creek. It was named the "So-Different." It *was* different from the majority of the other saloons in this, that it was headquarters for some of the most rapacious sure-thing "gamblingers" and high-graders in the State.

In the So-Different, the man who offered Hawke an opening was a fellow named Lee. He operated the roulette wheel. He looked Hawke over carefully, not seeming to do so, and evidently judged him to be a greenhorn. He asserted that he had been cleaned the night before by a mine owner and needed another bankroll to keep the wheel going. To anyone who would furnish the roll, Lee declared, he would split the winnings, fifty-fifty. Hawke furnished five hundred dollars, and Lee put the money in the wheel drawer. Hawke knew the So-Different for what it was. He knew it was cut throat or be cut, every man for himself. He kept his eyes open.

Shortly after Lee had put Hawke's money in the wheel drawer, Lee's partner, a club-footed man named Wagoner, hung around for a moment, exchanged a covert meaning glance with Lee, and left the room. Shortly afterward there entered a tall man garbed like a miner; he strolled about the room, paused by the wheel and began to play. Hawke was watching alertly.

The man played cautiously for a time, placing small bets on various numbers. Then suddenly he began to plunge, to bet the limit on certain numbers which are close together on a wheel. Into the pockets, opposite these numbers, the little ivory ball dropped so often that in record time Hawke's five hundred dollars had been won by the mining man; won from the wheel; won in apparently legitimate fashion, if anything about a roulette wheel can be called legitimate. Hawke knew there was something wrong about it, that the mining man was in cahoots with Wagoner and Lee; but for all his sharp watching he couldn't discover how the cheating had been done. They were trimming him, but they weren't going to get away with it.

Lee did everything he could to cover the real play, was very careful not to overpay any of the mining man's winning bets. He grumbled continuously about the Swede luck of the player. But he wasn't quite smooth enough. Hawke was to become, very swiftly, as hard and cold and rapacious as the worst of them, and he was cutting his eye teeth now, and his wisdom teeth. He saw that, after the ball had made several turns around the hollowed-out rim of the stationary bowl in which this wheel was set, and was about to drop into one of the pockets, Lee kept the wheel revolving very slowly, and kept his hard eyes on the ball. Sometimes, at that precise instant, the ball would stop suddenly, as if it had hit an obstruction, and would fall into one of the pockets. It was always one of the pockets opposite a number on which the plunger was betting.

The thing was done too smoothly, Hawke couldn't solve the puzzle. He knew Lee was a crook and a double-crosser, and that was enough for the present. He turned his back on Lee and walked into the next room, to the club-footed man, Wagoner. Wagoner was in charge of the faro game, and Hawke knew more about faro than he did about the wheel. There were some important things he didn't yet know, even about faro.

Remember, he was cutting his eye teeth now. And he thought that faro was the squarest of all banking games, that it was difficult for a faro dealer to cheat the faro players. So he put up some money in the faro game, and Wagoner, being certain he was a greenhorn, gladly took him in.

Hawke seated himself in the lookout chair. Two or three miners had come in for a drink at the bar, and Wagoner opened the game for them. Before he had finished the second deal, another man entered and made two or three small bets. It was the mining man who had won Hawke's five hundred dollars from the wheel. Hawke's sharp eyes saw the man signal with his fingers and saw Wagoner signal back; the mining man laid a ten dollar gold piece on the king, which won on the next turn. Hawke felt his temper rising. Even the faro bank was crooked.

Calmly Hawke leaned over, drew out the money drawer, and shoved its contents into his pocket. Wagoner started and stared at him, and asked him what in the hell he thought he was doing. "Grabbing my money while the grabbing's good," Hawke retorted. "Before you throw it off, like Lee did at the wheel."

Wagoner remained motionless and rigid. His thoughts were eloquent in his eyes. He was wondering whether or not he had better go for his gun. In a hair's breadth of time he decided against that act. Hawke was innately cold and calculating, and he was mad as a hornet right now. He was embittered and reckless. Wagoner saw in his face that he was in a most excellent mood for a fight, would even welcome it, and to hell with the odds. The dark face was ugly, the black eyes dangerous. He was perfectly capable of creating a good deal of damage if Wagoner dared to start anything with him. Wagoner was not a fool. He shrugged and turned back to his game.

Hawke stayed right there until after the game closed, and still he stayed. He wasn't going to leave till he got all his money back. There was still to be retrieved that which Lee had taken at the wheel. As a last resort, there was the Colt inside the waistband of his trousers. But any man could pull a gun and hold them up, if he had the nerve. Hawke yearned to do it with finesse. His vanity was pricked again. They thought he was a sucker, a greenhorn, a come-on. Temper and vanity together urged him to show them that he was quite as smooth and sophisticated as they. He had for the first time come into contact with a crooked roulette wheel and a crooked faro box, but he was a long way from being the green fool they thought him, and they were due to learn that fact.

Shortly after the faro bank had closed, into the gambling room came a grafter known as "Spit-out Bill." Spit-out Bill started a poker game. At first there were but three hands in the game, Spit-out himself and two miners playing. Then, very casually, Lee came strolling around, shot a veiled glance at Wagoner, and both of them took hands in the poker game.

With his face as expressionless as a leather mask, his black eyes as hard as flint, Hawke dropped into a chair to the left of Spit-out Bill. Those significant words *spit-out* spoke eloquently to Hawke. As he slipped into the chair, both Wagoner and Spit-out Bill calmly drew their six-shooters and laid them on the table in convenient positions. The display was doubtlessly intended to intimidate the man they believed a tenderfoot. Hawke ignored it, with a grim grin to himself. How well he knew he could whip the Colt from the waistband of his trousers and fire it before either Wagoner or Bill could snatch one of those guns off the table. He realized to the full that he was walking right into a trap the outfit had laid for him, that the outfit was an ugly one, that he was in a dive in the heart of the red-light district, that his life wasn't worth a counterfeit cent if he made a careless play; but he never batted an eye.

He had not taken the chair to the left of Spit-out Bill by accident, but by design. Spit-out Bill had a device which he used in his grafting, a device which he called the bug. It was fashioned of a section of clock spring, to which was riveted a double clip of the same material. The bug was fastened to Bill's left thigh, after he sat in the game. In this device he would slip his hold-out cards. When he was ready to use them, he would drop his hand to his knee, turn his head to the left, twist in his chair, slightly—to the left—and spit. As he straightened in his chair he drew his hand up his thigh and drew with it the cards waiting in the bug. Spit-out Bill. And Hawke had heard of Spit-out Bill before.

He knew that the bug must necessarily be within plain sight of the man sitting at Bill's left. Spit-out could not operate his graft unless a confederate was sitting at his left hand. Lee and Wagoner were men from the roulette wheel and the faro box. Poker was not their especial graft, they were leaving that to Spit-out Bill. And Hawke was sitting to the left of Spit-out Bill. They played for an hour, and nothing of any note occurred. Wagoner depended mainly on marked cards, and he was an expert marker. He used a camel-hair brush and made his marks on the backs of the cards with inks of various colors. He had become so familiar with those marks that he could read the cards by watching their backs as he dealt, almost as rapidly as he could have read them had he been laying them down face up.

Shortly after the game started, Wagoner tore up the old deck and demanded a new one. Hawke made no sign. Just a little play ostensibly to indicate to the greenhorn that Wagoner was square. But Hawke saw him reading the marked cards every time he dealt. So, every time Wagoner dealt Hawke politely stayed out of the jackpot. He had a little graft of his own. With the wheel and the faro bank, he had been playing their game. They were playing his game now.

They had started this, let them take what was coming. Hawke proceeded to play up to their idea that he was a greenhorn. His most significant act in this direction was in shuffling. He would hold the deck in his left hand and mix the cards with his right, shoving about half the cards down between the others. Now and then he would attempt to shuffle the deck in the ordinary way— and make a very bad job of it indeed. Then, with a muttered curse at his own stupidity and clumsiness, he would pick up the deck, place both elbows on the table, and proceed with his "hay-mow shuffle." The hay-mow shuffle appears innocuous enough—to one who knows nothing of its possibilities. It seems a most awkward and inexpert method of shuffling cards, seems to prove eloquently that the shuffler is anything but poker-wise.

But—appearances deceive. The expert hay-mow shuffler can run up two hands with it, and that in less time than it takes to perform an ordinary shuffle. Hawke was an expert at the hay-mow. He had been practicing it for an hour or more every day ever since he had first learned it back in the junction city.

Now, opportunity walked right up and smiled at Hawke. One of the miners shoved a big bet into the pot, and the pot was already very large. Lee and Wagoner, as well as Spit-out Bill, were tense with interest and exultation. This was going to be a big haul. Lee hesitated, apparently debating whether or not to call the miner's bet. Hawke picked up the discards and began to shuffle them idly. No one paid any attention to him; it was a very natural act, it was Hawke's deal next. Before the play was finished in that hand, Hawke had run up two hands in the discards. He picked up all the cards for his deal, gave the deck a false shuffle, crimped it and laid it down for Spit-out Bill to cut. Shark though he was, Spit-out cut the deck neatly to the crimp.

Lee had won the last pot. He sat opposite Hawke. He thought things were running beautifully. The betting began to zoom. The two hands Hawke had run up he dealt to himself and Lee, to Lee a queen-full and to himself an ace-full. By some "lucky chance" Spit-out Bill got a drop-in that for some reason proved very expensive to him. At the final showdown there was more than a thousand dollars in the pot, and the showdown lay between Lee and Hawke. Lee had four hundred dollars on the table in front of him. Hawke tapped him. That is, raised Lee till Lee bet his last cent. Face up, Hawke laid down his winning spread.

Then, very quietly, Hawke pushed his chair back from the table. He might have to shoot his way out of this, but he knew his draw. That face-up hand told the tale. Not a man said a word. Hawke raked in the pot, with his left hand. He proceeded to stuff gold and bills into his left- hand coat pocket. The right hand was poised, motionless and ready for action. His black eyes dared every man at the table to make a move. Not a man did. They sat silent, scowling and staring at him. He cashed his checks and calmly walked out of the saloon.

The next day he met Spit-out Bill on the side-walk. And—Spit-out Bill grinned and held out a hand. He chuckled. "Say, that was a good one you pulled last night. Damned if you haven't got nerve, going up against three birds like me and Lee and Wagoner. What's the matter with you and me doing a little business?"

Hawke talked things over with Spit-out, and he learned about gambling from him. He learned that Lee's wheel was a "needle wheel." Set in a rim around which the ball ran was a needle-like piece of steel—the needle. This needle was connected by wires with a loose nail set in the table in front of the dealer. The dealer could work with a confederate and throw the ball into the pocket opposite any number on which the confederate bet, by the simple act of pressing down his thumb upon the nailhead and throwing the needle into the track of the ball. He learned too that Wagoner was an expert "squeezer," that he was dealing with "The Old Thing" out of a double-box, or "Sand-tell," as the crooked boxes were called. But he learned also that Spit-out Bill was a born double-crosser, and he passed him up.

Now Hawke made the acquaintance of a noted squeezer named Sam. Sam was an expert dealer of the Old Thing, the Odd, and Wedges. Sam was smooth, not crude and unfinished like Wagoner. He knew and could operate all the devices known to a crooked faro dealer. Hawke and Sam formed a partnership. They were two smooth experts together, but Sam *would* drink. And once he was thoroughly inebriated, he was a dangerous man to have behind the box. He was apt to fumble and disclose the fact that he was pulling two cards from the box at once, or to expose his cards unduly when he was dealing the Odd. But Hawke decided to take a chance.

He sent to Denver and bought of a sporting goods store a double-box and suitable cards with which to deal the Old Thing and the Odd. Sam coached him, he practiced and became proficient so that he could take Sam's place when Sam drank too much. He knew he had to be proficient. It would take much sheer cold nerve to squeeze down the lever with his left thumb while he "pulled two" out of the widened slit in his trick-box, all under the concentrated, suspicious gaze of a dozen or more players. Those players would take him apart limb by limb if they caught him making a crooked move. Therefore he made his proficiency the acme of finesse, as he did everything, and he and Sam went on the road.

They moved to Gunnison, but they lost their house in the saloon there because one of the saloon owners was a faro bank fiend. He insisted on bucking the tiger in spite of all Hawke could do to prevent it, and lost so much money that the other saloon partner ordered Hawke and Sam to move on. They moved west to Crested Butte, a coal mining camp north of Gunnison. Sam made a drunken blunder there and they could get no more play. Hawke quit him in disgust, and took the trail alone again. But Sam had served his purpose, as had Spit-out Bill; through the agency of those two, there wasn't much about gambling that Hawke didn't know. He was now become the finished product of his years. He was grim, cold and relentless, rapacious and worldly-wise. He was out for the money and cared little how he got it.

He went next to Pueblo, a town considered good by saloon men and gamblers. At Pueblo were three smelters and the big steel works; the town was the center of a large farming district, it was wide open and had been for years, was filled with the riff-raff that had drifted in from many States. Verily a good town for Hawke. But he did not want to get into another gambling house, he wanted to get on the inside with a house of his own. He had no difficulty in finding a suitable location, a saloon belonging to the brewing company and for lease by them. It was situated on Union Avenue, near one of the gambling houses and close to the red-light district. In reality, the place would have been a gold mine for any man who was of a caliber to harmonize with the surroundings. Hawke was not such a man. He was a man of strange contradictions. See this: a very large percentage of the trade there came from the prostitutes and their satellites. If Hawke could have mingled with them and been one of them, he could have coined money. But he couldn't mingle with them. To him they were miserable creatures.

The women were merely "damned chippies," and the men were "sons of blankety blank Macks who lived off the earnings of the women." And, poker face that he was, he couldn't quite conceal his contempt for them. They sensed it, they felt it, knew he considered himself far above them in the social scale. Social scale! Yet, he told himself, morally he was no better than they. He was after money regardless of the fashion of getting it. So were they. Yet, between him and them was a sharp dividing line. He knew it and they felt it, and his business dwindled to nothing.

He set his jaw, and mentally told them to go to

hell. He wasn't so bad as they. Damn it, he wouldn't live off a chippy, he'd make his own money and in a man's way. He wouldn't double-cross a friend, a partner, not even a sucker who trusted him. He wasn't as they, and they could keep their filthy money. Burning with indignation, he moved what was left of his stock to Red River, New Mexico. He did not go alone. He took with him another man of his own age, who had made a failure of the same business in the same town for the same reason. The man's name was Charles Glassgow. He was tall, with tow hair, hard blue eyes and a smooth, fair face. He was remarkably cool, not easily roused to anger, but a very dangerous man once he was aroused. He was Hawke's kind of man.

Charley didn't like rubbing elbows with the chippies and the Macks, either. Hawke welcomed his company, and made a partner of him. Crook, gunman, desperado of the worst sort, wild and lawless a character as ever lived in the Old West, Hawke was; but one singing word vibrates like a crusader's call all down the long corridor of his life—*clean*. Whatever he may have done, whatever crimes he may have committed against the law and against society, never once did he violate that word. It is in his face today. There is a devil in the black eyes under the jutting white brows; mouth and chin, lines and planes, form the face of a man who has lived hard, who has been cold and reckless. But from brow to chin, out of all the years, there is no stain. From the soul out he's clean as a whistle. He saw the same thing in Charley Glassgow.

So with Charley Glassgow he went to Red River. They made a worse failure there. For Red River was a booming mining camp and there was nothing substantial behind the boom. Their saloon failed and they went broke. Glassgow took it philosophically.

"Well, Hawke, looks like it's up to us to throw our feet," he suggested. No use to tackle anything here, but we've got to hold up somebody. We've got to have money. The owner of the big store has got *dinero*. So has this other saloon man. But they both know how to keep it. What say we stick up one of the placer mines?"

Hawke said it was all right. They decided to go to Elizabeth-town, a mining camp on the east side of the range. The next day would be the Fourth of July. Most of the miners would be in Red River celebrating. Before sunset, avoiding the stage road and the cabins of prospectors, they arrived in the vicinity of the big hydraulic plants above Elizabeth-town. They paused behind a clump of stunted cedar and surveyed the workings on an open hillside sloping toward them. The slope was gashed with numerous bedrock drains leading to the huge pits where the huge nozzles had been at work. But Hawke decided it was no go. A shotgun guard was patrolling the line of sluice boxes. The gunman of contradictory character made a self-revelatory remark: "Nothing doing here, Charley. We might have known we'd find the mine guarded. I don't care to put myself in a position where I'll have to kill a hard-working man for his money. Let's go farther upstream. If we find nothing that looks good we'll go down and stick up one of the E-town saloons."

"I'm with you," Glassgow replied. "I'm no more of a killer than you are."

They traveled a mile and passed two more guarded mines before they found a layout that looked good to them. There was no one here patrolling the sluice boxes. But the place was not entirely unguarded. Smoke came from the chimney of a cabin across the gulch, and the smell of cooking food drifted on the breeze. They didn't want to show themselves, so they decided to wait till night and clean up the gold from the sluice boxes without arousing the man in the cabin. They were extremely hungry by the time darkness fell. The pit opened toward them, and was more like a huge open cut than a pit since there was no bank on the lower side. On that side were rows of heaped boulders. Between them ran the ditches in which the sluice boxes were installed. For some reason the miners had left part of the usual head of water running through the sluice boxes.

Once the man in the cabin came out, walked over to the edge of the cut, surveyed the workings below and went back to the cabin. Shortly afterward the light in the cabin went out. Apparently there was but one man there, but Hawke and Glassgow were taking no chances. Glassgow was to keep an eye on the cabin while Hawke jerked out the block riffles and prepared to rob the sluice boxes. He turned the water running through the four-inch hose into the ditch where the boxes were, got a pick from a pile of tools close by and began to pry out the wooden blocks forming the riffles in the upper box. Before he had the blocks out, Glassgow joined him. He had found no sound of life about the cabin and had come down to help Hawke. Cleaning that long string of boxes was a big job, and it was to their advantage to finish their task with all possible speed and be out of there.

Glassgow had barely set about aiding in the work, when a curt order came from a man standing on the rim of the cut between them and the cabin: "Say, you down there! Stick 'em up before I fill you full of buckshot!"

Hawke dropped his pick and darted to cover behind the second box. Charley leaped behind the stone monument which was foundation for the framework holding the giant. The man on the bank fired both barrels of his shotgun. Both Hawke and Glassgow returned his fire, drove him back from the ridge. Hawke ordered Charley to stay under cover while he himself slipped around and got in back of the man on the rim. The man on the bank fired again before Hawke reached the mouth of the drain. He had changed his position. Hawke raced across the gulch, turned upstream on the other side and doubled back, which brought him out above the cabin. The maneuver had taken several minutes, and while Hawke was accomplishing it three other men ran up from the direction of Glassgow's rear and captured him before he was aware of their approach.

As Hawke passed the cabin, he heard voices in the cut, and promptly retreated behind the building. He saw the dim outlines of four men approaching, and heard Glassgow say hotly: "I didn't have any pardner, I tell you. I was going it alone."

"He's lying fast as a horse can trot," an angry voice interrupted. "I tell you I saw two of them down there."

"Well, it doesn't matter," one of the others replied. "We've got one of them, and we'll soon get the other. I know both of them. They used to run the Elkhorn Saloon."

Hawke scowled and cursed under his breath. But he remained motionless until the men filed into the cabin with Glassgow. The first one in lighted a candle. As the last man entered the room and started to close the door, Hawke rounded the corner of the cabin, set his toe against the door and walked in, his gun leveled and cocked.

"Up! Reach for the ceiling, all of you!"

Startled, the miners obeyed. The man with the shotgun hastily laid the weapon on the plank table and put up his hands.

"Now, line up against the wall!" Hawke commanded. "Charley, see what they've got."

Charley was not slow to obey. He laid upon the table the loot he had taken from the miners, a bulldog revolver, a bill-fold stuffed with bills, and some small silver. At Hawke's orders, Glassgow pocketed two hundred dollars in bills, leaving the remainder of the loot lying on the table. Then, while Hawke kept the miners covered, Glassgow rifled the cupboard and took a supply of bacon and cooked food.

"We're not going to tie you up," Hawke told the miners. "We need a stake to help us out of a bad jackpot, and this two hundred does it. Behave yourselves with caution, and you'll get your money back, every damn cent of it."

"Fair enough," replied one of the men, a twinkle in his eyes. "You're welcome to the loan—if you'll leave the sluice boxes alone."

"We'll let 'em alone," Hawke promised. "Much obliged. Come on, Charley."

Be it recorded that the miners did behave themselves with seemly caution, not even stepping to the door to watch the holdups go. And be it also recorded that they got their money back, not long after, when Hawke's faro game was running.

Charley and Hawke made a hurried departure from Red River. They kept to the high trails close to the backbone of the Sangre de Christo Range, and stayed away from the railroads. They reached a branch of the Denver and Rio Grande Railroad and stole a ride in a box car to Pueblo. There they went to a hotel, washed up and considered the next move. Charley suggested that they look for a job. Hawke shook his head. "Nix on the job, Charley. No more jobs for me. I worked my head off on the last one, and what did I get out of it? I'm going after money."

Glassgow shook *his* head. "Not me, Hawke. I've had my fill of this kind of life. I'm going to take the first job I can get, and stick to it."

He meant what he said. He took the first job he could find, unloading coal cars for a big coal company—*at five cents a ton.*

And again, Hawke took the trail alone. He ran into an ex-railroad man, a fellow named Al. Al had a proposal to make, and he was very reckless indeed. He was flat broke and out of a job. More, he was suffering from a malignant disease which could be cured only by a long term in a hospital. He needed money and he was desperate. He proposed that they hold up the Bessemer bank. Hawke objected. A getaway from the bank would be difficult. So they looked about, and decided on holding up the Greenlight gambling house. This was situated above a saloon on Union Avenue. The Santa Fe railroad track ran alongside the building. There was a stairway leading from the back door of the big gambling room to the lot back of the saloon. From it access was easy to the alley and to the railroad right of way.

There were things to be considered. That back door was kept securely fastened by a heavy padlock and chain. There were a dozen or more dealers in the Greenlight. It was certainly conceivable that some of them might put up a fight. Hawke laughed at Al's fears. The dealers, he said, with his mouth set and his eyes hard, would regret it if they put up a fight. The back door wouldn't hold two seconds. It was a joke. The panels were so thin he could kick a hole through them with one well-aimed blow. They planned the robbery for that night. Al secured from a second-hand store two worn jumpers and two old caps. They made themselves look like miners as much as possible. They smeared their faces with soot, and did look like men who had just come off shift. They hid themselves on a vacant lot across the street from the gambling house, and waited for the policeman to pass the saloon and proceed on his way to the lower end of his beat. When the officer was out of sight, they crossed the street and went upstairs to the gambling room.

They shoved the door inward and entered the room together, both men with their guns drawn. Hawke ordered those inside to line up against the wall, with their hands high against the wall and with their faces to the wall. As one of the faro dealers left his table to obey the command, Hawke saw him reach down and push a button. While Al was taking the money from the tables, the porter from the saloon answered the bell, thinking the faro dealer had rung for drinks. The porter was a big colored boy, and he stopped at the door, his eyes popping, as Hawke swung one menacing gun upon him. With a gasp of surprise, the colored boy leaped backward, fell, and sprawled the full length of the stairs.

"Beat it, Al!" Hawke snapped. "Hell's going to be popping!"

Al obeyed, snatched up all the money he could hold and leaped for the back door. He kicked out the panels, crawled through the opening and went down the back stairs at perilous speed.

Hawke stepped over to the wheel table, thrust one gun into the waistband of his trousers, and took a handful of bills from the drawer. He was furiously angry. They had planned that, if such an emergency arose, Al was to stand at the back door and keep the room covered till Hawke joined him. But Al evidently saw fit to look out for himself, and left Hawke to face the music alone. Hawke backed to the rear door. There were forty men or more in the room. Keeping them covered with one gun, with the aid of his left hand he crawled backward through the hole in the shattered door, then turned and leaped down the stairs. As he reached the porch and ran for the alley, someone opened fire on him from the back door. He raced down the alley and took to the railroad track. By now several men were following him and firing wildly at him. None of the bullets struck him.

He evaded his pursuers by darting into another alley, and by many devious turns he made his way back to his room. To his astonishment, Al was there. And he had with him, heaped on the table, all the money he had got at the gambling house. It amounted to something over four hundred and fifty dollars.

Hawke buried his loot in an old ash dump. He felt certain some of the dealers had recognized him. The police officers kept close watch on him for a while. Al went his own way. To cover his departure, Hawke worked for a while for a contractor who was doing some excavating for the water company, then he dug up his loot and drifted to Trinidad. He found nothing there to attract him, and returned to Pueblo. There he found that Glassgow had gone into the saloon business, and Glassgow told him of a man who had been a successful counterfeiter. This man agreed to furnish Hawke with a pair of metal moulds for the making of silver dollars. But the man failed to produce the moulds, took the money Hawke had put up, and quietly faded out of the town.

Hawke attempted to make moulds for himself out of plaster of Paris, then tried making them out of copper by the electrolysis process. Neither attempt was successful. Hawke gave it up in disgust and hit the trail for Arizona. It was a long trail he took now, with a team and wagon he had bought, and with camp utensils for use on the way. Via Walsenburg, he followed a branch of the Denver and Rio Grande Railroad, through a pass into the San Louis Valley southwestward to Taos. Of which route he makes an interesting remark; it was usually traveled by Kit Carson whenever he went from his home in the ancient pueblo on the Rio Grande to Bent's Fort on the upper Arkansas. From Taos Hawke continued southwestward through the mountains to Santa Fe and on to Albuquerque. The going was bad. Much of it was through loose sand. In many places the team was mired in the sand and Hawke was forced to unload the wagon before the horses could get it free. It was hot work under the New Mexican sun. Hawke tired of it and threw away everything he could do without.

Even then, the horses were exhausted when he reached Holbrook. He sold the animals, his harness and wagon, the whole outfit, for fifty dollars and beat his way by freight train to

Prescott. Broke again. More poker. Prescott was wide open. It supported thirty-two saloons. For a gambler, it was a good town. Hawke played heavily and the exchequer grew fat again. His phenomenal ability to win attracted the attention of the assayer of the Mud Hole mine, a man named Anderson. The assayer was a poker fiend, but he was no fool. He wanted to know how Hawke did it. Hawke read him for a man with daring. He showed him how to make the hay-mow shuffle, how to deal from the bottom of the deck, how to cap the deck. Anderson was an apt and eager scholar. He grew proficient. He and Hawke departed on a trip to Phoenix.

The place was infested with grafters, but Hawke and Anderson cleaned up a good stake, then returned to Prescott and cleaned up some more. But by this time people in the district discovered that Hawke and Anderson won altogether too much. The two were barred from the games. Which worried them not at all. Their pockets were handsomely lined. They departed for Cripple Creek.

In Cripple Creek, Anderson shrewdly planned to use his capacity as an assayer. He would set up an office and buy glommings from high-graders. Hawke might have profited by that move, but he refused it then. He returned to Pueblo.

Again now he felt the urge he had felt before. Damn this grafting business anyhow, and holding up other gamblers. It was a silly cut-throat business. He was going to quit it, get a job and live an orderly life. He did get a job, ditch digging. The season was summer. The sun was hot. The air in the bottom of the deep ditches was like the breath from a blast furnace. The workmen sweated profusely and drank continuously. The water they drank came from the Arkansas River. It was contaminated with the sewage from Florence, from Cañon City, and from all the other towns on the upper Arkansas. Hawke went down with walking typhoid. When he got up again he was emaciated and weak. He couldn't work.

He decided to go to Cripple Creek and join Anderson. Anderson was now a leader of one of the most daring gangs of high-graders that Cripple Creek ever knew. He made occasional raids on his fellow crooked assayers. He was concerned at seeing Hawke so worn by the ravages of walking typhoid. Anderson suggested that they hold up a few saloons. They proceeded to do it, with such ease and so little dramatic contingencies that there is no interest in recording the robberies. With his pockets well lined again, Hawke went to Florence. It was well for him that he left Anderson. What guided him no one can say. But his whole life shows a peculiar trail of evasions of dire consequences. Perhaps the answer lies in the phantom cowpuncher who rode ahead of him down the ridge in Wyoming that time he broke

188

out of the jail in Lander. Here it was again. He left Anderson just in time. The man was caught taking sacked ore from a freight car and sent to the reformatory at Buena Vista.

Now Hawke contacted and joined a Cherokee of mixed blood, commonly called "The Indian." The two of them staged several holdups. Again these are of no pertinent interest here. Hawke, of the complex character, conceived a vast dislike for a man who was in charge of the power plant. The man was notorious for his cruelty and brutality. To the men under him he was a slave driver. It was known that he beat his wife and children, but no one had the daring to try to stop him, or to risk death and injury by taking the meanness out of him. Hawke and the Indian decided to take him down a peg.

On the night of pay day, when the man was coming to town, Hawke and the Indian waylaid him. The Indian commanded him to halt. The man ignored the command and laid the whip to his horse. Hawke leaped into the road, snatched the horse's reins and dragged the animal to a stop. One of the shafts of the buggy struck Hawke in the right side and cracked a rib. That didn't stop him. It served only as fuel to his already flaming temper. Gunman, desperado, reckless, crooked gambler; but he hated men who beat women and children and horses. To abuse a woman or a little child was to invite the swift and devastating rage of Hawke Travis. As Hawke yanked the horse to a halt, the man in the buggy cursed furiously and began beating at the Indian with a long whip.

"Don't shoot, Ed!" Hawke cautioned the Indian. "Let me at him."

The Indian answered with a savage curse as the whiplash again descended on his head. He sprang onto the hub of the wheel, dragged the man from his seat and slammed him to the ground. Hawke shoved the Indian aside, gripped the man's coat collar and jerked him to his feet. The man had little money, but they took it. Then they turned the horse loose, and hitched the man into the buggy. They strapped his right arm to the right-hand shaft and his left arm to the left-hand shaft. They both of them climbed into the buggy. Hawke picked up the whip.

Poising it ready to strike, he addressed the man hitched in the horse's place. "Now, Mr. Wife-beater, we'll see how you like some of your own medicine. Get up, and trot along smartly. One yell out of you, and I'll lay you out cold." And he brought the whip down in a stinging cut across the fellow's shoulders.

The man was thoroughly cowed. He grunted with pain, but he did not yell. He went forward, expending all his strength, dragging the light buggy up the road. Hawke and the Indian continued their joy ride for more than the distance of a city block. Then they got out of the buggy. Again Hawke addressed the man.

This is only a hint of what you'll get if I ever hear of your laying a hand on your wife and kids again. And don't forget it."

He and the Indian turned the man loose, left him to get home as best he could, and slipped off into the darkness. The next day the whole town was talking about it covertly. All over the town men winked at Hawke, chuckled and slapped him on the back, without a word to indicate the cause of their secret amusement. But Hawke knew. The Indian had thought the joke too good to keep. Results did not stop there. As Hawke was about to pass police headquarters, his victim stepped out of the door, accompanied by an officer, and pointed an accusing finger at Hawke.

"There he is now, damn him!" His voice was a snarl of venom. "Arrest him and hold him until I can get a warrant from the district attorney."

Hawke eyed the officer coolly. "You'd better think twice before you try to arrest me without a warrant. You know you can't do it, and so do I. If you have any intelligence, you realize that you must prove any charges you make against a citizen, or lay yourself liable to a judgment for defamation of character. If you think you can prove anything against me, go to it. I'll be somewhere along Union Avenue when you get back from the district attorney's office."

He heard nothing more about that exploit—from the police. But the town was buzzing with it, and his exploits would not bear the light of publicity. That night the west-bound passenger train carried Hawke toward Leadville, but it didn't know he was aboard. Now again that strange guiding hand, that something which watched over him, was on the alert. At a water tank above Cañon City the train stopped. Two men boarded the blind baggage. Each wore a long black raincoat, each had a slouch hat pulled down over his eyes. Hawke knew why they were there. They were going to hold up the train. But why did they just happen to board the coach platform where Hawke stood? At all events, they did.

If he stayed on that train, Hawke was getting himself into a dangerous position. He had a reputation as a gunman and desperate character. The fireman had seen him when he boarded the train in the Pueblo yards and had recognized him. Unless he had a good alibi, he would be taken in for complicity in that robbery. He got off the train, walked back to town, went to a hotel, showed himself noticeably, and went to bed. The next day officers were scouring the country for the train holdups. They did not molest Hawke Travis.

He moved on to Blackhawk. There was only one gambling house in town, owned by a cigar-store man, who had suffered a run of ill fortune.

Hawke proceeded to rig a needle in the bowl of the man's roulette wheel. Within the first week he won back all the money the cigar-store man had lost by unskillful playing, and took in a large bankroll besides. Naturally, the man began to love Hawke like a brother. They took in another man they both had known in Denver and opened two more gambling houses, in camps near Blackhawk and Central City. There is little to record here. Hawke picked up a stake and moved on to Denver. He took an interest in a poker game running above a saloon on Curtis Street. At the time, Denver was headquarters for most of the card sharks in the country. Cross-roaders made successful raids on mining camps and cow towns, and came to Denver to rest up and spend their money. Grafters of all kinds were everywhere.

Hawke got into touch with a gang which owned and operated a gambling house located at Council Bluffs, known as "The Big Store." The place was luxuriously furnished. It was not openly a gambling house. It was called the Millionaire's Club, and posed as a high-class place wherein was staged prize fight entertainment. Races were also run, or supposed to be run.

The men from this place hung about the gambling houses along Curtis Street. The habitués of the underworld flooded it. Hawke became known to them as a gambler and gunman as ruthless and as without conscience as the worst of them. He became known as a man, too, who would not double-cross, who had nerve, who was out for the money, and who would not squeal.

But Hawke himself was coming slowly and ever more surely to the parting of the ways. Experience had taught him that he could not expect from them trust for trust, that there was *not* honor among thieves. They would double-cross him, their friends, their partners, anybody, if the double-crossing meant money. Added to a latent desire for lawful life, to a growing realization of the profitlessness of his mode of living, was an involuntary contempt for crookedness born of crookedness. But the time was not yet for the turn in the trail.

Timberline was in Denver, Timberline the Cross-roader. Hawke knew him of old. He was tall and fair with innocent blue eyes and a smooth, boyish face. He looked, and acted, most exquisitely, the part of a greenhorn. He went about garbed as a teamster, and usually traveled about in a covered wagon. He was in reality an expert card shark, his especial graft being second dealing. It was his first appearance in Denver. He and Hawke got together, with an eye on a flourishing gambling house. The game keeper did not know Timberline. He had seen Hawke but once, the game keeper, so Hawke set about evolving a good disguise. For a week or more he did not shave.

On the night he and Timberline planned to clean the place, Hawke put on a suit of brown corduroy, heavy shoes, a white Stetson, a flannel shirt, and a necktie adorned with a nugget stick-pin. The dapper, well-dressed gambler was gone, in his place was a mining man. To complete the illusion, Hawke added for the occasion a few properties, a nugget watch-chain strung across his vest and several samples of rich ore to carry in his pockets.

Timberline put in an appearance at the gambling house first. He looked for all the world to be a greenhorn teamster, ripe and ready to be plucked. He sat in a game and lost a little money. An hour later Hawke strolled into the place. When the game closed the keeper had lost his bankroll. And the next morning the game keeper learned that he had been the victim of two of the cleverest card sharks in the West. He had a sense of humor. The next evening he opened his game, with a borrowed bankroll. On the wall back of his chair was pinned a spread of four tens and a jack. Beneath it was a piece of cardboard on which he had written:

"This is the hand I held. A sucker and his coin are soon parted."

Below this was another spread of four queens and an ace, and under that spread was another strip of cardboard on which he had written this:

"And this is the hand Timberline played— damn him!"

That blew things up for Hawke in Denver. He became too notorious altogether. He could get no possible chance to play. And what good is skill to a gambler if no one will play with him and lose money? He had about decided to leave Denver behind, when he ran across Mendelholt.

Mendelholt deserves a word, for sheer cussedness. A short time before, he and another man had figured in a successful bank robbery, at Salida. Mendelholt had risked himself but little. He had been posted across the street from the bank. His confederate came riding down the street. Mendelholt signaled that the coast was clear. The confederate, Ryan, left his mount in front of the bank, stepped inside and held up the cashier, who was alone because the other employees were out to lunch.

Ryan emerged in a very few moments, mounted his horse and went racing down a side street, fled across the bottom and up the Ute Trail. He made his escape, met Mendelholt later in Colorado Springs and divided the loot, slightly over five thousand dollars. Ryan was now in Chicago.

Mendelholt proposed to Hawke that they hold up one of the passenger trains running into Denver. He sent his woman down to the Union Depot to watch the messengers remove the money from the safes in the cars. So he got a line on the money being carried. They decided on the Missouri Pacific which arrived in the early hours of the morning. Mendelholt sent for Ryan. In Mendelholt's room, with the woman present, they worked out the details of the holdup.

The holdup was to occur east of Denver, within walking distance of Ryan's room near the outskirts of the town. They would secure dynamite from one of the powder houses northeast of the town. Hawke was to handle the powder while the others held up the train crew. At the particular spot they chose for the robbery, five miles east of the town limits, in barren country where no ranches were within a mile, all conditions seemed favorable. They went out and looked the place over and returned to Denver.

That night Mendelholt turned Ryan over to the police. The Bankers' Association had offered two thousand dollars reward for the apprehension of the man who had robbed that Salida bank. Hawke was infuriated and disgusted. Talk about double-crossing! Mendelholt had not once intended to rob the train. He had made the elaborate plot to lure Ryan from Chicago for the sole purpose of turning him in and securing the reward. Ryan was of different caliber. He took his medicine, he made no defense at his trial, and said nothing in any way to involve Mendelholt in the robbery. But the expression of his eyes when he looked at Mendelholt was eloquent of what he intended to do when he finished his seven-year sentence in the Cañon City penitentiary. He never had the opportunity of carrying out that wordless threat. A year later Mendelholt was killed in a saloon brawl.

But the whole affair served to increase Hawke's growing disgust with lawless life. Honor among thieves? What a large and mouthy jest! Ryan had had honor to the extent at least that he would not welch on Mendelholt. And Ryan was in Cañon City penitentiary. Mendelholt was free, with the money for which he had sold his pal. He would have sold Hawke as quickly, had the opportunity afforded itself. Hawke swore luridly. The only reason that he had not been trapped long before, or killed, was because his skill was so great, his gun play so fast that the others were afraid of him. They feared him to such an extent that life was growing tame. Somehow, this wasn't his idea of a good time.

He longed to find in life zest in the very living of it, peace and good will, the respect and liking of his fellow man, and some security. He had none of these. He had longed to become a gunman. He had become one, of such deadly efficiency that he did about as he pleased and seldom even had to draw his gun any more. He had wanted to become an expert gambler. He had achieved that, too. He was so expert that he could win anywhere he sat in. But he spent his money as fast as he made it, and life was stale and flat in his mouth. He sensed vaguely, now, that the thing that had lured him above all others, perhaps, was the battle, the fight for supremacy. The fight, the excitement, the danger, all these had lured him. His own achievement had taken them away from him, left them behind. And to turn to an orderly mode of living would be even more tame.

He didn't quite know what he was going to do about it. All of his calculations were upset. He faced chaos, in mind and heart, and didn't know which way to turn. Almost—almost to the parting of the ways. But not quite. Fate had in store for him another chapter or two of grim tuition, another experience or two, before the floodlight was turned on to illuminate the things he saw now only through a glass, darkly.

Not knowing exactly why he went, save that Denver was uncomfortably hot in more ways than one, he left Denver behind and went back to Cripple Creek.

There, with the idea in mind of turning over a new leaf, he got a job as trammer in the Ajax mine near Victor. His muscles were soft, he was still feeling the effects of typhoid fever. But his muscles hardened to the work and his vitality began to come back. He had no trouble in getting a job, since the union miners of the district were on a strike, though they were beginning to go back to work and the backbone of the strike was already broken. Seeing a chance to better himself, he quit the Ajax and went to work at the Independence mine. It was dangerous work, devilish underhand things were done during that strike. He saw one horrible accident originating from such cause. A wire cable snapped, letting loose a cage loaded with fourteen miners coming off shift. The cage dropped to the bottom of the fourteen-hundred-foot shaft. All but one of the men in it were killed. Hawke learned later, from the fireman on duty at the time, that the exhaust pipe from the hoist cylinders had been plugged by someone with fiendish intent, causing the hoister to lose control of his engine. This allowed the cage to shoot up into the sheave wheel, snap the cable and drop.

Someone blew up the Independence Depot, a man named Harry Orchard, then operating in the district. He set off a bomb that killed or crippled forty miners on the platform waiting for the train to take them home. Conditions became very bad indeed. Enraged by the outrages, strike breakers and their employers rounded up several of the trouble makers and escorted them from the district. There was a store where the idle miners were drawing supplies, presumably at the expense of the union. The strike breakers wrecked the store. All this, time, Hawke was attending strictly to his business, striving to make a reputation as an honest miner. But the work was killing, he was in constant danger between the two warring factions, his wages were small. In another revulsion of disgust, he began playing poker again.

His winnings often amounted to far more than his wages, but he wanted to make more money, and it was in sight. The boom days of the camp had long since passed. Most of the large deposits of rich ore had been worked out, but the Independence, the Portland, the El Paso and several other mines still were producing a considerable amount of rich sylvanite ore. Organized gangs of high-graders entered the stopes between shifts to cobb the rich ore from the waste. The glommings were bought by the owners of pseudo assay offices for from one-half to three-fourths of their value. Hawke abruptly decided to get in on it.

He and his partner managed to get away with most of the rich ore they opened up in their stope. They carried it off in their clothes, they cached it and carried it away a little at a time, they entered the stope between shifts through an abandoned shaft and carried off more. They cleaned up royally, until the company temporarily closed down the Independence while the workings was being laid off into blocks to be leased to independent miners. Then Hawke and his partner sought another mine where the glomming would be as good. They worked in the El Paso, several other mines on Beacon Hill and Raven Hill, and glomming was still good.

It was a difficult matter to convict a miner of glomming, even if he were caught with the goods. The condition was this: the big companies were considered fair game by the high-graders. Most of these companies were owned by Eastern or foreign stockholders who spent none of their dividends in the camp. The high-graders spent nearly all of their ill-gotten gains in camp, and nearly everyone winked at their activities. It kept money in circulation, it made good times, to have the money spent there. But the mine owners, of course, objected violently. Ore in place was classed as real estate, which could not be stolen except by forged deeds. But—once the ore was mined and sacked, placed in bins or cars, legally it became personal property. Thieves of personal property could be prosecuted for larceny. This was not often done. Usually, the miner caught at high-grading was discharged and his name placed on the blacklist kept by the secretary of the Mine Owners' Association. Once he was blacklisted, a man was done working in that camp.

Somebody blacklisted Hawke Travis. He never learned who had done it. He surmised it had been done by one of the spies hired by the association. The pertinent fact is that it was done, and that Hawke didn't care a tinker's damn. Why work for the mine owners, breaking his back in those dangerous tunnels, when he was in solid with the most daring high-graders in the district? From being a miner, glomming profitably on the side, Hawke turned again to utter lawlessness.

In one place in this record I remarked that

Hawke did not like a fight, that he did not welcome gun play and was sickened when he had to kill. In another place I stated that it was the fight and the danger of lawless life that lured him. The two statements may seem to be contradictory, but they are not. Like many statements which seem to contradict each other, they dovetail perfectly when correctly fitted together. He did not like physical violence, senseless warfare and bloodshed. But he gloried in conflict that pitted his skill, his intelligence and his shrewdness against that of other men. He had yet to learn that that conflict which challenged him to exert the best in him could be found in other paths.

He looked the situation over, and saw a good thing. The mine owners, in blacklisting high-graders, committed a tactical error; they would have done far better to prosecute them. Being merely blacklisted, the men were free to join the organized gangs levying their toll on the mines. They became a genuine menace.

Most of them, having once been miners in the very places they robbed, knew the lay of the ground. Most of them were on friendly terms with miners still working there. These working miners passed hot tips to the high-graders. Often before foremen or shift bosses knew that a large deposit of rich ore was "coming in," the high-graders had been apprised of it by some friendly miner. Before leaving town, the high-graders would don mining clothes, take along a lunch bucket, several candles, a prospecting pick, a few ore sacks—and a gun. No one paid any attention to them. They looked like miners going to work or coming off shift. Their graft was so organized that coats were made especially for them, coats in the capacious pockets of which it was possible to carry a hundred pounds of ore. They would take a long and devious route sometimes, but more often the high-graders were quickly in the mine and reached the stope they had come to rob.

The richest ore of the district usually occurred in the seams of phonolite dykes, smeared on slabs on both sides of the seam as if swabbed there by some gigantic brush. Occasionally the seams widened to pockets or huge deposits of jewelry ore, so called because of its phenomenal richness. One such deposit in the Independence mine, varying in height from fifteen to twenty feet, in length and width from fifty to a hundred feet, was known as the bull pen. Smaller deposits of this rich ore still remained in the different mines. It sounded easy, and it sounded good. To reach the mine unsuspected, directed to a rich spot by some friendly miner, to clean up all the rich ore broken out by the last shots, to look around for added worth in the vein that could be kicked out by a pop shot, to clean up with the drills and hammers some double-jacker had left there. If they were delayed until after midnight, simply cache their ore in some abandoned tunnel and remove it next night after dark. Yes, it looked easy.

But Hawke was to learn. Most of the rich ore had played out. Rich hauls were few. It was hard work and dangerous. The high-graders were forced to descend and ascend hundreds of feet of ladders. Many of the ladders they had to climb, because they were working secretly and must at all cost escape detection, were in old shafts and manways and were unsafe. Walls and roofs of the old stopes and tunnels through which they stole were in many places untimbered. In these places falling rock or a cave-in at any time might cripple or entomb the daring ore stealers. Old stulls, lagging and ladders were slimy and coated with fungus, and might pitch a man down through a hundred feet of space. There was danger of coming suddenly into a "dead end" where their candles would go out and the very air meant death. And some of the guards, sawed-off shotgun in hand, patrolled in the dark. Always the dark, underground, where a high-grader might suddenly run into a special guard deliberately laying in wait to trap him.

And sometimes after it all, all that work was for nothing. Perhaps someone had looted the stope before him. Perhaps the stuff they lugged away at the price of sweating labor and omnipresent danger proved to be fool's gold. Fool's gold is pyrites of iron and copper, and the rich sylvanite ore resembles it so closely that the difference in the two is not easy to distinguish by candle light.

Considering all these things, Hawke began to grow wary. He had about decided to abandon high-grading for some less dangerous way of making money. Then he and his partner had a tip concerning a haul to be made in one of the mines. They promptly acted upon it. As they were descending the ladders in an old shaft, the second section above the first level proved too weak to hold them. Water dripping from the surface had rotted the side rails of the ladder. It tore loose from the supporting stull. Its very rottenness saved them in some measure. It snapped into several sections, partly breaking their fall as they crashed onto the floor of the landing at the next level. The other man was below Hawke when the ladder broke. Hawke fell upon him. The other man fell in such a manner that he broke both bones of his left leg below the knee. There were no miners near, this mine in which they had fallen had been abandoned years before. The lower workings of the old mine connected via a long tunnel with the shaft of another mine. That was the only way out, for the man with the broken leg.

Hawke must go down the ladders to the tunnel, through the tunnel to the shaft, up the manway to the shaft-house—to the night watchman. He cut some splints from an old powder box and bound the broken leg as best he could. Then he rose.

"I'll be back with help to get you out of here as quickly as I can," he said, and added grimly, "if the damned night watchman doesn't drill me the minute I climb into sight."

The other man shook his head quickly. "You don't take any such chances for me. We ain't got an ounce of glommings on us, but they'll know what we were here for." He motioned toward his broken leg. "You help me, and I can make it to the next level. I can get down the ladder with your help."

"I get you," Hawke interrupted quickly. "I figured we'd have to carry you out of here, but if you've got the guts to do that, we can probably reach the landing of the May-Pole shaft. There's an electric hoist there, and I can run it. And the layout's different. I can get the drop on the watch-man there."

"I've got the guts," the other man asserted. "Just try me."

Hawke went ahead when they reached the ladder, supporting and aiding the other man. They managed to reach the May-Pole shaft, but the other man's suffering was terrific. Hawke climbed to the shaft-house, and stepped from the collar of the shaft, a handkerchief across his face, his gun drawn. The watchman was astounded by his sudden appearance, too astounded to make any protest. Hawke disarmed him and tied him, got the injured man up and took him to the nearest station on the electric line running between Cripple Creek and Victor.

Neither of them had been recognized. There was no kick-back from that affair, save that both men were done with high-grading. Yet, of all the money Hawke had made in that hazardous enterprise, none remained. His disgust growing, he decided to make one final stake there and get out of Cripple Creek. He began looking about for an opportunity.

There was in town a man named Cameron who ran an assay office, so called. He had been buying ore from Hawke and the other high-graders. He forced the high-graders to take as low as fifty per cent of the worth of the ore. Halcron, another high-grader, was enraged at Cameron for his rapacious practices. Halcron proposed to Hawke that they rob Cameron's office. The crooked assayer had accumulated a large amount of ore which he intended sending to Denver in a day or two. It was Cameron's custom to reduce the ore to powder and place it in a huge iron chest. He kept the chest fastened with three heavy padlocks, and boasted that it was burglar proof, that no one could get into it without arousing the whole town.

While Cameron was pleasantly occupied in playing poker in the back room of Billy Moore's saloon, Hawke and Halcron entered the assayer's office by way of the back door. Now, Cameron himself often worked late at night, and he made considerable noise with blast furnace, mortar and bucking board. Therefore, with the lights on and Cameron himself apparently there, nobody paid any attention to the noise going on in Cameron's office. Halcron watched in the alley while Hawke cut through the three padlocks with a hack saw. They carried off three hundred dollars worth of ore. Hawke had his stake. He went alone and afoot from Cripple Creek.

At a crossroads town he found Timberline. The two joined their fortunes. They went to Leadville in a covered wagon, then on to camps in the Southwest, gambling, winning stakes and losing them. They finally brought up in the mining camp of Sonora, Mexico. Business was good, and money easy.

One night Hawke was playing poker in the back room of a *cantina*. A Mexican constable came in and took Hawke by surprise while he was raking in a pot of money. The constable jammed a Colt against Hawke's ribs and told him that he was arresting him for holding up the S. P. train near Stein's Pass. Hawke knew better than to make any foolish moves. The Colt was against his ribs, he was caught off guard, and the constable was venomously angry because he himself had lost considerable money in playing poker—with

Hawke Travis. He accused Hawke of being the notorious Black Foley, who was known to have participated in the Stein's Pass robbery.

Hawke paid little attention to him. He paid as little attention to the excitement caused by his arrest. The constable knew very well that he was not Black Foley. He herded Hawke to the *calaboso* and proceeded to search him, to take from his pockets something over five hundred dollars. Hawke laughed at him sarcastically.

"Your game's the surest in the long run, *amigo*. I win fifty dollars off you playing poker, and you win five hundred off me playing your game. But listen." His cold black eyes probed the Mexican's face. "Did you hear how much *dinero* the express company lost in that holdup on the pass?"

The constable watched him closely. "*Carambe, si*! More than fifty thousand pesos. Eh, *are* you then Señor Foley?" His face was blank with astonishment.

"I thought you knew it all the time," Hawke said smoothly, his one concern for the moment being to make the Mexican believe that he was Foley, after all. "But I'm hardly fool enough to say very much to you, to incriminate myself. And I don't feel like talking until after I eat. I might talk turkey then, if you act reasonably."

All of which was noncommittal and veiled, but the Mexican read it as Hawke meant that he should. He fetched the tray of food, and Hawke demanded to know how he was going to eat while he was wearing handcuffs. The constable promptly removed the bracelets. Hawke told him to set the tray down by him. He had seated himself on the cot in the cell where he had been placed. The Mexican obligingly put the tray by Hawke.

In the same instant Hawke sprang up, swinging his doubled fist in a mule kick punch to the officer's chin. The constable went back, half unconscious from the jar, and thudded to the floor. Hawke leaned over him, thrust a hand into his pocket and jerked out the keys the officer carried. He knew the street would be filled with miners, cowboys and Mexicans. He dared not wait to search the fallen constable for a gun, and he had no idea what the man had done with his own gun. He leaped to the barred door, unlocked it, dashed out and turned down the street. Someone fired at him from the front porch of the *cantina*. He went at a run toward the low hills to the south of the town. Before he reached the edge of the timber clothing the hills, he heard the drumming of hooves behind him and doubled his pace.

He reached a brushy draw, and followed it to the top of the range. He had effectually escaped his pursuers. He went down to the open plain, and on to the El Paso and Southwestern Railroad. He did not chance boarding a train till the evening of the next day. Arrived in El Paso, he borrowed money from a gambler friend to last him for a few days, and sat down to think things over.

Dead ahead of him was the parting of the ways, but he did not know it yet. He only knew that, in looking back over the last few years, his disgust rose to monumental proportions. All of the philosophical thoughts he had known from time to time crowded his head. Discontent fermented in his brain. Again he asked himself, what was it all getting him? He had helled around, robbed, gambled and killed, he had made money in quantities, and spent it as fast as he acquired it. He had nothing in his pockets now but a few dollars, borrowed.

He did not believe in a Divine Providence overseeing the world. He could see no evidence of one, from his point of view. Nature, he told himself, was a murder scheme. Life was continually destroying other life to promote its own growth. Why, he wanted to know, should destruction be the dominant law of the world? He thought it was. What possible good could come to anyone or anything in the last analysis from all this senseless destruction? He had himself been a harsh instrument of destruction. What had it got him? Nothing. His wife was long gone, out of his life forever. His child was dead.

He felt himself wince at that. Then he cursed himself for wincing. It was folly to grieve for the dead. Grief couldn't help the dead, it could only injure the Jiving, himself. He'd best keep his thought on doing something worth while. But what would that be? And how should he go about finding it?

Maybe the Philosophical Anarchists were right; they held that it was wrong to use force to accomplish their ends. Again, maybe the Individualists were right; anything you did was permissible, according to them, as long as you developed your own individual consciousness. No, he decided, they were both wrong. Even democracy wasn't able to establish justice between man and man, humanity being as it was. Perhaps a wise despotism would be better. The masses were too selfish to be fit for true democracy.

And he scowled, and cursed, and wondered what in the hell was the matter with him anyway. He certainly was doing some wild and weird thinking. But he couldn't lay hands on himself, couldn't probe the cause of his discontent. There wasn't any Providence, and there wasn't any law, capable of solving *his* problem—unless it was the law of cause and effect. "As a man sows, so shall he also reap." Was that it? Damned if he knew. It must be so. It was up to every troubled man to work out his own salvation, and Hawke Travis was certainly a vastly troubled man. But still he didn't know what he was to do about it.

He was restless, nerved to a high pitch of

rebellion, dissatisfied beyond expression at the emptiness of existence. He wasn't certain what he was going to do. Go back to Denver, maybe, and trim some poor sucker out of his money. And spend the money, and trim somebody else. There was no zest any more. The suckers were too easy. He was too polished and finished a crook. He was tired of the whole damn business.

Abruptly he realized that he had stumbled upon the key to the whole situation. That was it. He was tired. Very tired. Tired in body and brain. He had been living at a frightful tension. What he wanted was a chance to hole up somewhere off by himself, in some corner where he would be undisturbed, where he could rest and not be continually on the lookout for prying officers and maddened suckers whom he had trimmed. It would have to be some place where no one would know who or what he was, where no one would dream that he was a desperate character, and gunman and professional gambler. Where he would be looked upon as a respectable citizen, and consequently left to his privacy. But where the devil was there any such place in the West? He certainly wasn't going to leave the West.

Since his intelligence was alert and shrewd, it pounced upon the ideal place for his retirement, and that with very little effort. He thought of the ranch in the cove. It was still his, half forgotten, lying there idle through all these years, in the very heart of the Colorado Rockies. If there was any place to which he could go and step into an alien world for a while, it was to the ranch in the cove.

He was always a man of abrupt decisions, and his decisions once made were usually unalterable. He must keep for expenses the few dollars he had borrowed. So he stole passage on the train from city to city. Stopped en route to trim a sucker at poker, felt better with his pockets a little fuller, and stole more rides on the train. The last few miles of the journey, he walked. He knew more than anything else a feverish desire to get back to the ranch in the cove, to rest. He was off his feed. That was all there was to it. He'd rest up, get himself in prime condition again, then off for Denver—and let the suckers beware. But he wasn't thinking so much of that future now. He was conscious only that he must get to the ranch in the cove. Perhaps the phantom puncher was the answer to that, too.

At all events, he reached the ranch in the cove with the least possible delay. He found the conditions of the valley changed. New families had come in and settled there. The ranch in the cove was typically an old abandoned ranch.

The cabin was somewhat dilapidated, but he cleaned it up and moved into it, mended the roof, and looked about.

It took him several days to do that, and already he felt better. In looking about he was surprised at what he found. The fruit trees he had planted were sturdy and big, all of them bearing, apple, pear, plum and cherry. There were still some apples on the apple trees, and evidence under the other trees of what they had borne. All the orchard needed was pruning, and a reasonable amount of care. He set to work ridding the trees of suckers. Even the currants and gooseberries he had planted had multiplied and grown. It took him several weeks to clean up the orchard and berry bushes. It was a pity he couldn't be there in the spring to prune those trees and put them in proper shape.

He sat in his cabin in the evening and thought about it. He was surprised to realize how much better he felt. He strolled out into the clearing, looked up at the big pines in the yard, and at the star-sprinkled sky. With a start he realized something else. For the first time in his hectic years, he was at peace. He was content. He was even happy, tending growing things, things that were his own. There was no one to bother him, no officer at his heels whose very presence was a menace threatening to drive him on. No poor sucker, maddened at losses, ready to make wild and foolish plays and force him to yank out a gun and shoot somebody. Really, it was restful in the biggest sense of the word. Why shouldn't he stay till next spring?

The longer he rested, the more cool his nerves would become. The more fit he would be to turn back to Denver and bust the old town wide open. He abruptly decided he *would* stay till spring. There was a tie camp up in the hills, perhaps the same company for which he had cut ties there so long ago. His money was about gone, the provisions he had bought needed replenishing. He'd go to town and stock up. When his money was gone, he'd work in the tie camp for the winter, come back and trim up his fruit trees, and then—what? Oh, yes, Denver. Denver and the suckers, ready to drop into his hand like a ripe plum. So he made his plans, feeling the surge of new vitality, body and brain keen and alert again. He stood at the parting of the ways, and did not know it.

He went to town for provisions. Since he was going to stay there for a while, it might be well if he acquired speaking acquaintance with his neighbors in the valley. He went out of his way to do it.

These people then in the valley may be, so far as Hawke knows, all living or all dead. In any case, there is no knowing what their reaction might be to seeing their names in this record. Therefore, every name here used shall be a fictitious name. Beyond the names, we stick to facts. They appear here exactly as Hawke found them.

There were two families for whom Hawke had little liking. Or, rather, there was one family and one man. The family was the Cross family. Buck Cross was a tall, gaunt man with a sharp, predatory face and a crafty, predatory nature. The Cross ranch lay northeast of Hawke's ranch in the cove. Cross had two sons, Bill and Jerome. Hawke had no use for any of them. Mrs. Cross had been dead for a couple of years, and the men kept slovenly bachelors' houses. Hawke passed the time of day with them, read them with his sharp black eyes, and knew them for what they were.

Due north of the ranch in the cove lay the ranch of the other man Hawke did not like. This man we'll call Boone Trench. Trench was tall, rather striking in appearance, his hair unusually curly. "Curly" was one of his nicknames. Hawke's knowledge of people was wide. And he knew Trench the moment he laid eyes on him. Trench did not know him. But Hawke happened to know that Trench was an ex-convict who had returned to Colorado after serving a short "jolt" in the penitentiary of an adjoining State. He had filed upon an abandoned homestead. This land lay near the western end of the valley. The valley was at the eastern base of the Rockies. Cross had much favored Trench's presence. Trench was in a way a rather notable character. He was decidedly handsome, good company, jovial, a good singer, a regular hoe-down fiddler. Graceful as a panther. The kind of man to command, without trying, the good graces of women. These things, naturally, had little to do with his being favored by Cross.

Trench was sly, crooked as a dog's hind leg, ready for anything, and shrewd about covering his tracks. Under his handsome, suave exterior, he was as rapacious and predatory as Cross.

It took Hawke no time at all to see that the Crosses and Trench openly resented his presence in the valley. Trench's place lay between Cross's ranch and the foothills to the west of Cross. The ranch in the cove lay between Cross's ranch and the main range in the hills, to the southwest. Just why Cross resented his return to the ranch in the cove Hawke could not yet divine, but he knew that it was so. He put his mind to the problem. Those springs which flowed out of the bluff south of the cove *might* be the answer. Cross pretended that they were. They furnished most of the water for the stock which ranged in the foothills west of the valley. But thinking got him nowhere, and Hawke decided to do some investigating. Up on the mesa south of the cove someone else had taken up a ranch. Hawke decided to go up there and call, to see if those people also felt toward him the open hostility evidenced by Cross and Trench.

He found the ranch on the mesa thrifty and well tended. He walked up to the door and knocked. A little old woman, thin and wiry, energetic and bustling, with a lean, shrewd face lighted by sharp, twinkling eyes, opened the door and surveyed him with hospitality and curiosity.

"Good morning," Hawke greeted her, doffing his hat. "I'm Hawke Travis. From the ranch in the cove. Come up to get acquainted."

"Top av the mornin' to ye, lad!" The little old woman threw wide the door. Her voice burred with brogue, as Hibernian as the name she gave him. "We're the O'Briens, and mighty glad to see you. We'd been wonderin' who'd took up down there. Come in, come in, and make yourself to home. How are things going with ye?"

Hawke stepped into the room, smiling in spite of himself. The little old lady was patently so friendly and kindly that he warmed to her. Here indeed was a different sort of person from the Cross outfit. He took the chair she offered him, determined without delay to sound her reactions to those fellows down in the valley.

"I've been so busy getting things in shape that I haven't had time before to get acquainted with my neighbors," he explained. "Cross and Trench haven't exactly received me with open arms. I am pleased to meet with a different reception here."

Kit O'Brien (Hawke later learned that everybody called her Kit), scrutinized him with her shrewd and penetrating eyes. "That's because you're honest, I reckon. And partly because ould Buck wouldn't welcome anybody who settled on the ranch in the cove."

"I gathered as much, Mrs. O'Brien. But I haven't been able to understand why."

Kit O'Brien shrugged. There was no dissembling about her. She was Kit O'Brien. She said what she thought, exactly when it pleased her, and if you didn't like it you could do the next best thing. She smiled. "Faith, that's easy, lad. Ould Buck needs the fine range back of your place for his stock, and he needs the wather from thim springs. Others have tried to settle that ranch in the cove, me lad, but they didn't make it stick. Buck Cross could tell you why. I like the looks av ye, and I'm tellin' ye without mincin' words. He'll have both range and springs for himself, for he's the kind to take what he wants, and he can't get the ranch in the cove, because somebody owns it, has owned it for years, and won't sell it. Maybe ye didn't know that. Maybe ye thought it was just some old abandoned place, as others thought and tried to settle there. Well, it's abandoned right enough. But the felly that owns it still pays taxes on it. Nobody around here knows who it is, but if ye want to stay there I'm tellin' ye, ye want to make some kind of arrangements with that felly, and ye want to watch out for Buck Cross."

Hawke nodded, smiling. "I happen to be the man who's been paying taxes on the ranch in the cove, Mrs. O'Brien. If Buck Cross thinks he can run me off my own place, he has another think coming."

"Well, by all the Holy Saints!" Kit's eyes popped. "I thought you wasn't any ordinary nester, lad. You're too smooth and polished like. We don't have many gintlemen here. Well, well! So the owner of the ranch in the cove has come back."

"He has," said Hawke impulsively, a grim glint in his black eyes. "To stay!" He caught himself up at that, with an involuntary start. Now, why in the devil did he say that? He knew very well he had no intention of staying, only until spring, till he had the fruit trees pruned, and was thoroughly rested and cool-nerved again, so he could go back to Denver and trim the suckers right. But he did not correct himself. Let it pass. Besides, Kit O'Brien gave him no chance to revoke what he had said. She beamed at him, leaned over and slapped a friendly hand on his shoulder.

"Good for ye, lad! We need a fighter in that valley. A fine young buck like yourself, to run out Trench and the Crosses, and make the valley a dacent place for a white man to live. Stick to it, we'll all back ye. But, mind, Buck Cross will be up to divilment the minute he knows he can't run ye out. It's queer he hasn't been sayin' somethin' already."

Hawke frowned slightly. The little old woman was positively charming, but was he letting himself in for something? He smiled to himself. His hair was graying at the temples, the drooping black mustache had more than one thread of white. Still she called him lad. Well, perhaps he was lad to her. And then again, though his first reckless youth was behind, he was still a young and vigorous man just entering his prime. Her enthusiasm made him feel alive again, stirred his blood to the old call of battle. Drive him off the ranch in the cove would they? He laughed aloud.

"He already has, Mrs. O'Brien. He was laying the law down to me yesterday. He told me he'd have me arrested if I used a drop of water from those springs for irrigating purposes. He claims the water, because, during heavy rains, it runs strongly enough to reach his ditch a half mile below the cove. I laughed in his face. He knows very well he can't hold the springs, because they rise on my place and because he has never filed on them."

Kit O'Brien grew excited. She leaned toward Hawke, her shrewd blue eyes flashing. " 'Tis little the ould divil cares whither or no he has any right to thim. And it's high time someone was showing him he can't run the whole country. Ah, if my Tim was here, he'd show Buck Cross!" The bright blue eyes dimmed. "My Tim is dead. He was a fightin' Irish divil. And me two byes are like him, Terry and Pat. They're out now irrigatin' the west field. They ought to be at church, but the weather's so hot 'tis necessary to kape the wather runnin' day and night. They've no use for

223

Buck Cross, or for Boone Trench, but I don't want to see 'em mixed up wid thim. They're only byes. Yet, if ye need help in fightin' that Cross faction, they'll give it to ye wid my blessin'."

"Thank you. I may need help before I'm done with Buck Cross. Hard to say. And I'm not entirely satisfied with the explanation that it's my springs which are the cause of his belligerency. There's something deeper behind it, Mrs. O'Brien. And I intend to find out what it is."

Kit nodded her head vigorously. "That's the way, lad. Go after him! That ould divil's liable to do anything. But ye needn't go? I'd like to have ye stay and meet the byes."

"Thanks, I'd like to." Hawke had risen, and half turned toward the door. "But I'll meet them another time. I must be getting back."

"And I'd like to have you meet Sally."

"Sally?" Hawke's black brows raised.

Again Kit O'Brien nodded. "Me niece, Sally O'Brien. She stays wid me. But she's gone to visit some friends in Arkansas Junction, and may not be back for a month. She's studyin' to be a teacher. Sally's independent as they make thim, and don't like to be beholden to her relatives. She's a fine girl."

"I'll wager she is, being your niece," Hawke returned gallantly.

"Go on wid ye! Ye leaned over the wall and kissed the stone, by the looks and talk av ye. Go on wid ye. But come back and see us again soon. The byes and Sally will be fair tickled to meet ye."

With a good-natured laugh, Hawke took his leave, promising to come again soon, and walked away in the heat of the Sunday morning, his heart warm toward Kit O'Brien. Kit was surely all right. He did come again. He came often, and met Terry and Pat. He liked the boys. They were fine sons of a fine mother, and plainly they liked him. Friendship grew and cemented between him and the O'Briens. Then, a month was gone, and he met Sally. Sally's hair was as black as his own, her eyes clear blue. She was tall and slim and straight, the kind of girl to make a man think. But it was Kit O'Brien who made him think, when he was there one afternoon, some two months subsequent to his first call. Terry and Pat were out in the field, and Sally had gone out to see them on an errand. Kit welcomed him in delight, and they sat for a while talking over the situation in the valley.

Cross had made no new move. "I fancy he's lying low, to see what I'm going to do," Hawke hazarded. "And I'm no nearer now than I was at first to his real reason for wanting to keep anybody off the ranch in the cove. Well, I'm waiting. I'll show them a thing or two yet, if they try to start anything."

Kit beamed approval. "They'll start somethin', never fear. Ye'll have your hands full one av these days. The byes'll be in pretty soon. But it was not thim ye came to see, I'm thinking?" There was a glint of mischief in the sharp blue eyes.

Hawke chose not to understand her meaning. "Yes, I did come to see the boys. I've been grubbing out sage-brush. I thought maybe I could get them to do some plowing for me. I believe I'll plant a little garden in the spring."

Kit hooted. "It's no use trying to fool me, lad. I have eyes in me head. For the life of me, I can't see why Sally wants to teach school. I'd rather she'd jist stay here till she's ready to go to the priest wid some likely young gossoon."

Hawke got abruptly to his feet. The conversation was getting too personal for him. Hat in hand, he turned to the door. "I've a lot of work to do," he said hastily. "Tell the boys what I wanted. I'd be very glad to have them do that plowing. I'll see you again soon."

Hawke's face was somber as he strode back to the ranch in the cove. Kit O'Brien was shrewd. She had caught the look in his eyes when he gazed at Sally. Sally *was* a girl to make a man dream dreams. But what right had he to such dreams? Sally O'Brien was at least twelve years younger than he, young and sweet and fair, with the best of life ahead of her. He was battle-worn and war-scarred, known among his associates of the underworld as one of the most cold-blooded, most rapacious and ruthless gamblers and killers who had ever escaped the noose. He thought of the things he had done, the robberies he had committed, the suckers he had trimmed, the men he had killed. Right now, they could slap him in the penitentiary for the things he had done, if they could catch him and prove them on him. No! It wasn't to be thought of! Him and a girl like Sally O'Brien. He knew he'd have to watch his step. He was uneasy when he recalled the look in Sally's clear blue eyes when they rested on him, the slight flush that, lately, was called so easily into her fair white face if he looked at her too intently.

Very certainly, he *must* watch his step! He must keep in mind that, after he had pruned the fruit trees, and rested a while longer, and showed Buck Cross and Boone Trench where to get off, he was going back to Denver, raring, to trim the suckers as they had never been trimmed before. He had met the parting of the ways, taken the fork in the road, the parting lay behind him, but he didn't know it.

Sally herself was a complication by virtue of her very character. She was high-tempered, fine and just and wise. Serious-minded, she wanted a home, a man of her own and all that went with him. If she realized that he had lived very wildly, and Hawke shrewdly suspected that she did, she evidently had an inner hope that he had decided to "quit his roaming and settle down."

Well, he'd be gone in the spring, and she'd forget easily enough. His task was to see that she had no reason to build dreams around him.

Resolutely, he put Sally O'Brien out of his mind, paused in front of his cabin and thought of his quarter section. Back of the cove was a tract of wilderness, ten miles or more wide and twice as long. In the tract was abundant feed for a large herd of stock. He couldn't help thinking what a splendid home a man could build there. He had thought that long ago. He thought it even more now.

Terry had told him that Buck Cross asserted he had been losing stock, that there were night riders in the valley and that he would like to find their hangout. Hawke smiled to himself. He was beginning to suspect Cross's real desire to keep anyone out of the ranch in the cove. A bold move, that! to complain of rustlers. Cross probably knew plenty about that rustling. The stock belonging to the valley ranchmen, most of it, ranged in the tract back of the cove. With someone settled in the cove, it wasn't so easy for a night rider to run off any of that stock. Yes, things were beginning to clear a little.

Before the end of that month, Buck Cross moved. There was no proof at all that Buck Cross was guilty of the depredation. But Hawke knew. He went to town on an errand. It took him several days. He came back to find his cabin gone.

Nothing remained of it except charred embers and an oblong spread of ash. He stood and stared, his temper surging. Then he whirled away and hurried to the O'Brien place. He explained to Kit in terse, bald words, and asked her to lend him some blankets, food and cooking utensils. All of the O'Briens were furious at the outrage. All of them knew who had done it. But they could prove nothing. Hawke dared say nothing—without proof to back him up. Such a move as that was exactly what Buck Cross was yearning to force him to commit. Kit O'Brien lent the things he needed, gladly, and asked what he intended to do.

"Build another cabin," Hawke told her violently. "I'm getting mad!"

He was. He was mad as a hornet. For a time he forgot all about going back to Denver and trimming the suckers. He camped that night under one of the big trees in his yard, a piñon that had shaded the cabin. The next morning he began construction of a new cabin, on the site of the old one. Some of the limbs of the tree had been scorched, but it was surprisingly undamaged, and its shade was an ideal spot for a cabin. For weeks, with the aid of Terry and Pat, Hawke worked as hard as he had ever worked, hauling in spruce logs from the bluff south of the cove, erecting the structure of his house. He built it larger and better than the old one. As it neared completion,

Sally O'Brien came down from the mesa to praise and admire.

The day the cabin was finished, Buck Cross moved again. Hawke had bought of the O'Briens a sturdy little horse. His cabin was finished. He slept in it for the first time. The next morning he found his horse shot through the head. Raging, he went up on the mesa to talk it over with Kit and Sally. He was getting in the habit of talking things over with Kit and Sally. Sally was outside somewhere, but Kit was in the kitchen kneading bread. Hawke walked in and sat down by the table. She looked at him in surprise, waving a floury hand and demanding to know what was wrong now. Hawke told her.

"It looks as if I'd have to give that Cross outfit a dose of their own medicine, Kit. I hate like the devil to destroy property. But that outfit needs a lesson. How am I going to work? I intended going up to the tie camp for this winter. But I don't dare leave my place for more than an hour or so. As surely as I do, they'll burn my new cabin, and maybe chop down my fruit trees. And they're so infernally slick that I can't get a thing on them."

"Ye need a wife, lad." Kit's eyes twinkled at him. "If there was someone at the cabin, the Cross outfit wouldn't come near. True, they shot your horse when ye were asleep. But they'd not dare try anything like burnin' the cabin again if there was someone there when ye was gone. They'll take no chances on being caught at their divilish work."

"Say, that's a thought, Kit. If I had someone there when I was compelled to be absent. But who I'd get is more than I know."

Kit frowned slightly. Queer, the boy liked Sally, all right. But he kept himself deep within a shell. He made no advances, though he must have known Sally would welcome them. Well, she'd better mind her own business. She said quietly, "I know someone who'd be glad to come up and stay at the place while you're gone. A nephew of mine, Jerry Maloney, who lives in town. He's an orphan, and he has but one leg. He lost the other hoppin' freight cars at the yard. He lives wid his uncle, my brother. The bye is a smart little divil. He'd be fine for ye."

Hawke thought that over for a moment. "Well, I don't know," he said at last. "That might be a wise idea. My temper's up. I'm determined to put Buck Cross in his place before I leave this valley."

"Leave the valley!" Kit turned to face him, her hands motionless on the bread dough, something very like consternation in her eyes. "You're leavin' the valley?"

"Why, I was going to the tie camp to work for the winter," Hawke evaded swiftly. "I must have money to keep me going, you know."

"Money!" Kit scoffed. "To hell wid the money, lad. Our ranch is thrivin'. We have all we want,

231

and plenty to sell. And the little ye'd use durin' the winter would be nothin' at all. Don't ye go leavin' that cabin that way, don't go leavin' that place to the mercy of Buck Cross. Ye stick right there, and I'll have Jerry come out from town to stay wid ye and be at the cabin when ye must be gone for a short while. I'll stake ye to grub for the winter. Now, now, say nothin'! I'll never miss it. Ye stick right there and fight Buck Cross to a finish. Why, ye'll be doin' the whole valley a favor! Can't ye see that?"

Hawke gazed at her silently, something hidden in his somber eyes. "You're white as they make them, Kit. I'll make no promises. But at least, I will stay for a while yet. We'll get Jerry out, if he'll come. If he'd like to live on a ranch for a while."

"If he'd like to! Lad, that bye's crazy for a ranch. He's a perfect fool about chickens and pigs. And he's fair wild to own a gun. He'd be happy just to look at thim two ye've got down there. 'Tis lucky they weren't in the cabin when it was burned."

"Yes." Hawke didn't tell her he carried his guns when he went away. He rose to leave. "Well, we'll see. But if Jerry will come, I'll see that he's in no danger from Buck Cross and his outfit."

"If he'll come!" Kit laughed. "Jist lave it to me."

Below the O'Brien ranch on the mesa was the ranch of Speed Jones, stockman and banker, good friend of the O'Briens, speaking acquaintance of

Hawke Travis. Hawke went to him, told him that he needed a team of horses and a light wagon, and hadn't now the money to pay for them. He looked Jones straight in the eye, and waited. Jones showed his hand rather plainly as he answered:

"Yes, I heard that your horse had been shot, and that your cabin had been burned. I also heard that—ah—anyone who thought he could drive you out of there was going to find something he wasn't looking for." Jones paused. Hawke said nothing. He knew very well where Jones had got his information. Kit O'Brien. Jones went on: "I have a pair of ponies in my herd, not prime stock, but not scrubs by a long shot. I'll have them brought up. I've three or four wagons I'm not using. Take your choice. Pay me any time. In fact—" Jones' voice became a drawl. "You know, I certainly hate skunks. There must be some in the valley. We get the odor sometimes clear up here on the mesa. Bad. I'd give a couple of ponies and a wagon any time to get rid of that stink. That's making you a proposition." And Jones grinned.

"You've come to headquarters," Hawke replied tersely.

The next day Hawke drove the ponies to town. When he returned he brought with him freckle-faced Jerry Maloney. The boy was thirteen years old, wiry and thin, abounding with vitality. Hawke had carried a forceful letter from Kit O'Brien. The crippled boy had, as Hawke himself expressed it, fallen for Hawke like a ton of brick. At the very thought of going to live at Hawke's ranch, he was wild with delight. The boy's aunt and uncle needed nothing more than Kit O'Brien's letter, but they were influenced by the boy's sudden and violent liking for Hawke. Jerry was welcome to go. So he went. Hawke wasn't surprised at the boy's liking for him. Boys and dogs always liked Hawke. Jerry was very enthusiastic about the ponies. Before they had gone two miles on the return trip, Jerry was driving them and calling them by name. As they passed the Cross ranch, Hawke called Jerry's attention to it.

"That's where the outfit lives, Jerry. The outfit we're going to buck, you and me."

Jerry scowled at the ranch buildings, and his freckled face spoke dire threats. He said: "They better not try to burn your house when I'm around. They must be a pack of hogs, trying to drive you off your place when they got a swell big farm like that."

Hawke nodded, watching the boy in some amusement. He was a likable little devil. "Hogs is the right term for them, Jerry, but it's a shame to insult a poor hog. But your job isn't active warfare against Buck Cross. If you have to fight something, you keep a lookout for the bobcats and coyotes. Then, there's a big dog-town below my place. Those little devils will sneak into my garden and play hob with it next spring, if you

234

don't clean them out." (Next spring? But next spring he was going to be in Denver, his gun thrust into the waistband of his trousers, giving the suckers the trimming of their lives, busting the old town wide open. Oh, was he?) "I'll have to teach you to use my shotgun."

"Aw, I shoot a shotgun, Mr. Travis! I'll show yuh!"

He made good his claim to efficiency. After they reached the ranch and had their dinner, Hawke brought out the gun, warning the boy that it kicked like a mule, and giving him some sage advice on the handling of the weapon. But his warnings were not needed. The boy had learned early and by hard experience; he was wise and shrewd, like a little old man. He was all over the cabin and all over the cove, getting about on his crutch as easily as if he had two good legs. For a few days Hawke was interested in showing the boy about the place, in studying him as a personality. To his surprise, one of the first things Jerry noticed was Hawke's fine and facile speech.

"Gee, Mr. Travis. I wisht I could talk like you can. How'd you ever learn to talk that way?"

"Oh, I used to teach school once, years ago," Hawke replied hastily. "That's nothing."

But to Jerry it was a great deal. He wanted to learn to talk like Hawke did, he persisted in saying. The result was inevitable. He had had little schooling, this boy, an ordinary school was not to his liking. Hawke was little short of a god in his eyes already. He would take anything Hawke said as gospel. Hawke led him out into the yard, and pointed to a brush-covered ridge north of the cove.

"Jerry, if you went over there looking for a stray horse, and found cigaret stubs and burnt matches lying about, what would you think?"

The boy looked up at him, his eyes sharp. "Why, I'd know right off the bat that some guy had been standin' there, watchin' the clearin'. And I'd know he didn't mean no good to anybody either."

Hawke laughed. "You'll do, son. You'll do. But, if you really wish to learn, say that you'd know he didn't mean any good to anyone."

It began there. Not many days later Hawke was telling himself that he wondered what some of the old timers in Denver would say if they could see him there in the cove, turned private tutor to Jerry Maloney. Somehow, he knew the old timers would never get a chance to laugh uproariously at that thought. When he went back to Denver he wasn't going to tell anybody what he'd been doing. Taking a rest cure, if they asked him. Oh, yes, he still intended going back to Denver. There were times when Denver and the wild old days seemed strangely far away. He didn't stop to analyze that. When he was back in Denver trimming the suckers again, the ranch in the cove would seem just as far.

VII

Hawke Travis had found a way of picking up a few dollars. In fact, he had picked up so many that he hadn't as yet had to call upon Kit O'Brien for the grubstake. That avenue of revenue was the piñon wood on his ranch. He found he could sell it in town. The ponies and wagon came into good use. A few weeks after Jerry had come to live at the ranch, Hawke was in town delivering a load of wood. He encountered Bill, the elder of the two Cross boys. Bill had taken on a fair load of whiskey. He came lurching out the door of Riley's saloon just as Hawke was passing. Boone Trench was just behind Bill. Young Cross turned and spoke to Trench, loudly, scathingly, manifestly intending the words for Hawke's ears:

"There the damned —— is now, Boone. For two cents I'd knock his damn block off."

Hawke's black eyes went cold. He reached into his pocket and withdrew his hand, extending it spread open toward Cross. On his palm lay two copper cents.

Bill stared at him. But instead of making any move to start anything, he began to curse, applying to Hawke sundry epithets calculated to make any man's blood boil. Hawke doubled his fist over the coins, made one leap and landed the fist flush on the point of Cross's jaw. Bill went down with a grunt and a gasp, knocked cold before he reached the sidewalk. As a fight, it didn't amount to much. Hawke turned flaming eyes on Boone Trench.

"If you want some of the same, hop to it!"

Trench backed off into the crowd of men that had poured out of the saloon. The day marshal came running across the street, and Hawke turned to face him coolly. The marshal scowled.

"Go on about your business, Travis. If I see you beating anybody else up, I'll run you in."

"Thanks. I'll try to see that you aren't around the next time it happens." Hawke heard some of the bystanders laugh as he went on down the street.

The next day he was in town with another load of wood. He encountered Kit O'Brien in front of the big general store. After she greeted him, the little old woman raised troubled eyes to his face. "I've been hearin' things, lad. I hear you're a desperate character, that—that you've been in jail, me bye."

Hawke felt his face whiten. His hard black eyes did not flinch. "Yes? Well, what of it? Who's been telling you things?"

"I'm not sayin'. Maybe it isn't so."

"It certainly is so. I nearly served time in Wyoming for half killing a fellow. My only regret is that I didn't make a better job of it. He needed killing."

Kit O'Brien sighed, and it was patent that the sigh was one of sheer relief. " 'Tis little I care how many men ye've killed. I was afraid ye'd deny it, lad. I might have known better, but I'm an old fool sometimes. No matter what ye've done, never be ashamed of it. Whatever rascals ye've killed, belike they deserved it. But the story is bound to hurt ye here, and somebody's started something else that will hurt ye more. They're sayin' that you're mixed up wid the rustlers who have been runnin' off the stock of the valley ranchmen, and that ye located at the edge of the hills to cover your movements. It's bad business, that story. And don't tell me it's a lie. I may be a fool sometimes, but I've sense enough to know that."

Hawke stepped close to her. "Kit, you tell me where you heard that."

"Sally heard the kids at the schoolhouse talking about it. She heard the Ewings talking about it at the table, too. Ye see?"

Hawke nodded. Since school had started, Sally was boarding at the Ewings, because the walk down from the mesa and up again was so long. Hawke stood for a moment thinking, then said abruptly: "Thanks. I'll finish my business and hurry back to the ranch. I have some purchases to make. I'll see you again, Kit."

His purchases were several boxes of cartridges for the frontier model Colt he had brought with him when he came to the ranch. When he arrived at the cabin that evening, Jerry stood and watched wide-eyed as he oiled and loaded the gun.

"Looks—looks like war, Mr. Travis."

"War to the knife, and knife to the hilt, son." Hawke turned his black eyes on the boy. "Something has happened, and I don't know what else may happen. This is no place for you now. You've got to go."

"But, Mr. Travis—" the words were an appalled wail.

"Don't argue, Jerry! Tomorrow I'm going to take you back to town. There may be very real danger here soon. I can't subject you to it. They're determined to drive me out of here, and they've found a leverage. There's no telling how far they'll go. You must be taken where you'll be safe."

The boy's chin quivered. His eyes were blank. It was as if a light had gone out of his face: Hawke turned away and went on oiling his gun; he didn't want to see it. After the boy went to bed, he paced the floor, consciously walking heavily, to keep from hearing the stifled sobs that came from the boy's bunk. But his determination was unaltered. The boy must go. He paced the floor for an hour or more, went out and walked about his yard, came back and paced the floor again. He found it difficult to force himself to go to bed. He had been furious many times in his life, but he had never been so furious as now.

He was not now enraged at some crooked

partner who tried to cheat him, or at some fool sucker looking for a fight, or at some unreasonable officer who wanted to put him in jail. He was enraged at a sly and organized band of crooks who were trying to oust him from his home. It was, doubtless, the most righteous rage he had ever known, and thereby the most devastating. In the heat of that hour Denver and its luring possibilities were as completely forgotten as if they had never been. He forced himself at last to sit down in a chair by the table he himself had made, and sat motionless, thinking. He heard no footsteps, was not aware that anyone was near the house until he heard a rap on the door. Cat-like, silent, he leaped to his feet, whipping out his Colt and leveling it at the door.

"Come in!" he snapped.

The door swung inward. Hawke started and the gun lowered. Sally O'Brien stood on the threshold. Her black hair was blown, her face very white, her eyes agonized.

"Mr. Travis!" She moved toward him a step, her voice tense. "You must get out of here. I heard Sam Ewing tell his wife that the Cross boys and Boone Trench are raising a mob to lynch you. They say they won't have an ex-convict and murderer in the valley. You and Jerry go up to Aunt Kit's for the night. Oh, don't stand there looking at me! They must be on their way right now. Wake Jerry and go!"

Hawke did not move. His face was as white as hers. "You know it's true that I've done time and that I've killed. Yet you come up here to warn me?" he said curiously.

"Don't waste words, and time. Of course I came to warn you. Most of the valley ranchmen will be in that gang. Cross and Trench have made them believe that you know too much about the rustling going on in the valley. They're coming, I tell you!"

"Well, let them come." Hawke's face hardened. "You are the one who must go, and take Jerry with you. You can keep out of their way by taking the trail along the bluff."

"You daren't stay!" The girl's heart was in her eyes. In a little rush she was face to face with him, and one hand was raised to grip his arm frantically. "You can't stay. They'll kill you!"

Hawke stood motionless and rigid. The girl's nearness shook him, and what he saw in her eyes. Grimly, in a blind flash, he reminded himself of what he had been.

"Let 'em try it! They may find I can do a little killing myself. Don't worry about me, Sally. Take Jerry and go. I'll waken him."

The girl stepped back, looking oddly old and beaten. Behind Hawke, a voice raised: "I won't go! They're comin' up here to try to kill you, and you want to send me away. I ain't goin'! I can use that shotgun. I ain't goin'!" Jerry rushed to

Hawke's side, his tear-stained face distorted with fury, his crutch thumping as he leaped.

Sally's eyes flamed again. "Good little brick, Jerry. If he *will* stay—Jerry! You *can* shoot. If they hurt him, kill them. Kill them!" The girl whirled and was gone at a swift run.

Hawke turned slowly to look down at the boy. For a moment he stood motionless, then he crossed the cabin and came back with the shotgun and a handful of shells. "These are loaded with buckshot, Jerry. If they show up, wait till they get within a hundred yards. We'll put out the light and step outside. You stay behind the big piñon."

The boy gulped and nodded. His face was very white. The freckles stood out on his skin in clearly defined small brown blotches. Hawke blew out the kerosene lamp, and the boy followed him out of the house. He placed Jerry behind the piñon and left him. It was some time before he heard the sounds of light footsteps in the brush back of the stable. He stood listening, his cocked Colt in his hand. He heard the whispering of voices. Two men were within a rod of him. He caught the scent of kerosene, and at the same instant one of the men stepped from the brush, a bulky package in his hand. Their intent must be to set fire to the stable.

The figure of the man was dim, barely discernible in the faint moonlight. But it was enough. Hawke took careful aim and pulled the trigger. The man dropped his bundle, clapped a hand to his arm, emitted a cry of fear and dismay, turned and bolted back into the brush. Hawke snapped a second shot into the brush where he judged the other man to be. Both shots took toll. The two went crashing away through the bushes, cursing and moaning by turns. At the sound of the firing, someone shot from the timber north of the house. From behind the piñon the shotgun boomed. Jerry was on the job. Hawke grinned grimly.

"Go to it, son!" he called. "Give 'em hell."

It was hell for a few moments. The raiders tried desperately to kill the two defending the cabin. But Hawke emptied his Colt at the fire flashes, with the speed and accuracy that had made him feared of other gunmen, and Jerry fired the shotgun as fast as he could load it and pull the trigger. The battle did not last long. With several of their men wounded, the raiders withdrew in rout.

The next day early, leaving the boy at the cabin, Hawke hurried up to the O'Brien ranch. He was concerned to know whether or not Sally had succeeded in slipping back to her room without the Ewings becoming aware of her absence. Kit O'Brien answered that question with murder in her eyes.

"She did not. The Ewings caught her as she was crawling through the windy of her room, and they fired her out bag and baggage. They guessed where she'd been. What's to come av it, I don't know."

And Kit went on to explain how things were. The Ewings had made much of it, had slyly hinted at ugly surmises. It had got about that Hawke was a murderer, a rustler, a desperate character of the worst kind. And the girl had deliberately gone to the cove to warn him and save him from the men coming to lynch him. They, the Ewings, certainly couldn't have in their use a girl who was sweet on such a man as Hawke Travis, and they predicted darkly that the valley ranchmen would not favor any such person's teaching their children. Sally had come home to the O'Brien ranch, lugging her heavy grip, wet to the knees from crossing the ditch, worn out from the experience. She was now in bed, asleep from exhaustion.

Hawke went back to his cabin, as cold and mercilessly infuriated as a man well may be. He could not blind himself longer to the girl's regard for him. Neither could he blind himself to his unworthiness of her. The best thing he could do was get out of that valley, and get out quickly. He would do it—as soon as he had cleaned up the Cross outfit. It wasn't likely that they would try to raid him again. He'd shot them up pretty badly. They'd take another tack now. He could not guess what it might be.

They made no move for the next few days. Within the next week a sensational robbery was committed. Bandits held up the eastbound limited of the D. & R. G. Railroad in Ute Cañon, a narrow gash in the Colorado Rockies. It was an ideal place for a robbery, some eight miles long, isolated. No one lived in the cañon, there was not even a wagon road through it. There was no ranch even near it at either end—save the ranch of Boone Trench, a trifle over five miles from the southern end of the cañon. The robbery caused great excitement in the valley. The robbers, there had been four of them, secured a large amount of gold and currency from the express car and killed the messenger.

Hawke mulled it over with narrowed, hardened eyes when he heard about it. Oddly enough, the description of one of the robbers tallied minutely with his own description. The man was described as being of medium height, black hair and eyes, black mustache. He had been dressed like a ranchman. And Hawke Travis knew that there was no mere chance in that. The Cross outfit was making a desperate play to get rid of him.

It was two days after the night of the robbery that Hawke went up the wash west of his ranch after some cedar posts. Since he would be gone but a short while, he took Jerry with him. Near the head of the wash, up which ran the road, there lived an odd character, a man named Jed Dinkle.

He was a bizarre figure, stoop-shouldered and gaunt. Habitually, he wore tattered overalls, faded flannel shirt and run-over shoes. His hair reached to his shoulders, twisting into loose half curls, the color of tow. On his head he wore a battered old derby hat two sizes too small for him. His face was leathery and seamed. His pale eyes told the tale of wandering wits that had never quite returned. Hawke had struck up an acquaintance with him, had won his heart utterly by treating him as he would have treated any normal man. He stopped by Dinkle's cabin, and the queer old fellow came out to see what he wanted.

"Morning, Jed. Have you heard anybody go by here lately?"

Jed squinted his pale eyes. "Nobody but the Cross boys and Boone Trench. Dinged if I know what they been doin' up there, unless they was lookin' for some of the A Bar C stock. Where you goin', Hawke?"

Hawke said that he was going to pick up a few poles. Jed insisted on going along. It was perhaps two hours later that Hawke drew his team to a stop at the gate in his east fence, and stood staring at his buildings some two hundred yards above him. In his corral were Bill Cross, Buck Cross and Sheriff Anderson. He said nothing, but opened the gate, drove through, closed the gate, drove on up to the corral and halted his team by the bars, which were down. The three men in the corral had watched his approach. As he drew his team to a stop, Anderson stepped close to the wagon and said curtly:

"Get down, and watch your step."

"Yes? Just why? I'm in my own yard, and attending to my own business, which is more than you're doing."

"Don't get smart," Anderson snapped. "I'm here on business all right. So are Cross and his son. I brung 'em along as witnesses, and they're ready to swear to what we found buried in the litter back of your stable."

"Sounds interesting," Hawke drawled. "What did you find?"

"Enough to send you over the road," Anderson retorted, his eyes malignant. "If not to hang you. No use stalling, Travis. You know damned well what we found. But one package of bills can't be more than a fourth of your share of the loot. What'd you do with the rest of it?"

"Oh, cached it, of course," Hawke replied airily. He was thinking with lightning-like calculation. It was useless to start anything here. It was three to one against him. He could probably get a couple of them, but they'd doubtlessly get him too. And Jerry was certain to be hurt if there was any gun play. He had nothing to gain and everything to lose. He turned quietly to the boy. "Put up the team and go over to Aunt Kit's place, Jerry. I'll see you later sometime. There's no time to talk now." He leaped to the ground from the wagon. "All right, Anderson. Your trick."

Hawke's preliminary hearing before the local justice went like clockwork. No witness appeared in his defence. The evidence summed against him was black enough. His description tallied minutely with that of one of the train robbers. He was now supposed to be an ex-convict, known as a desperate man with a dark past. A package of bills from the loot taken from the robbed train had been found in his yard. After a brief presentation of the evidence for the prosecution, he was bound over to the next term of the District Court.

Two hours later he sat in his cell considering the circumstances. He knew but one man among the many enemies he had collected who could have looked so like him. Neither of the Cross boys, nor Boone Trench, could possibly have made themselves up to look like him. The Cross boys were both hulking fellows. Boone Trench was well over six feet tall, his very curly hair was a light brown, almost blond. But there was a man who had enough enmity for him to join others in an attempt to trap him, and be glad to do it. He was trying to piece it all together when the jailer stepped to the door, unlocked it and announced gruffly that Hawke had a visitor. Hawke looked up to see Kit O'Brien. He greeted her casually, and she replied with meaningless words, till the jailer had walked beyond earshot. Then she stepped close to Hawke.

"It looks bad, lad. I tried to go your bail, but the judge refused to take me. I heard ye tried to get Jones to go your bail."

"I did. He refused. Said it wasn't good business. Old Buck is one of his biggest depositors. He admitted frankly that he didn't consider me guilty, but he knows what I'm up against. So I paid him for his ponies and wagon, and told him to go to the devil. But you wouldn't understand that."

"I understand that you're in a tight place," said Kit sharply. "The evidence is so strong that they'll send ye to the penitentiary. Ye'll have no help from anybody. Anderson's under obligations to Cross, ould Buck helped to put him into office. There's but one way. Take it."

With a swift movement she reached under her coat and slipped into his hand a small slim package. "And when ye get to the ranch—ye'll find Jerry there, holdin' the fort." She backed out of the door and hurried away.

Close to midnight, Hawke walked across his own clearing. There was a light in his cabin window. Either the boy was up, or he had left the light burning for company's sake. Hawke strode to the cabin and reached out to rap on the door. He heard a startled movement within, and Jerry's voice: "Who's there?"

"It's Hawke, Jerry. Let me in."

A surprised gasp answered him. He heard the boy come thumping across the floor, and the door opened. Hawke started to enter, and stopped short. Sally O'Brien was standing in the middle of the room, her heart in her eyes.

"What are you doing here?" Hawke demanded harshly.

"Waiting for you," the girl answered. "We knew you'd be coming. Or at least I did, and Jerry suspected it. I knew Aunt Kit went to see you, and why. We have here Terry's Colt, oiled and loaded and ready. I can have you a good hot meal in a few minutes. That's all ready, too."

Hawke drew a deep breath and stepped inside. "I'll eat it cold. And—I'll not forget this."

He closed the door behind him, and the girl moved swiftly to set upon the table an appetizing meal that she had ready for him. He tried not to think. He could see no ending but tragedy, for himself perhaps, and surely for her. Neither of them spoke till he had finished his meal, wrapped up a parcel of food to take with him, rolled up a blanket and thrust Terry's gun into his waistband. Along with his blanket and food he took what extra cartridges were there.

"Take care of yourself, Jerry," he said as he started for the door. "I'm off for the tall timber. Sally, come out here a minute." She followed him out the door, he closed it and turned to face her. "The less you know of where I go the better. I am after that gang, of course. I may get 'em, they may get me. I may come back, and I may not. But, if I don't come back—" His left hand supported the blanket roll upon his shoulder. His right arm closed about the girl and held her tight. "Forget me—and take care of yourself." And he was gone into the night. If he heard the sound of a sob behind him, he gave no sign.

Shortly after daylight the next morning he stopped at Jed Dinkle's cabin. The queer little old man stared at him in wonder. "Yuh look all tore up, Hawke. Somethin' wrong?"

"You're damned right there's something wrong, Jed. They jugged me for the train robbery. I was slated for the pen, and maybe to stretch hemp, if I stood trial. I found a file lying around loose, and beat it. I want to know if there's been any travel along the trail up here lately?"

Jed scratched his head, striving to draw his scattered wits to the problem. "Oh, you say they're gonna send you to jail? I wouldn't let 'em. Me and you can stand 'em off. Me and you—"

"Yes, yes—" Hawke interrupted patiently. "You're a brick, Jed. But has there been any travel along the trail?"

"Why, yeh. Yeh, more'n I've seed in a month of Sundays. All in this last week, and I heered some jasper ridin' back at all hours of the night. I wonder what them guys is doin' up in Granite Canyon?"

Hawke caught him by the arm. "In Granite Canyon? Who's in Granite Canyon? How do you know?"

"Oh, couple of fellas, camped up there. I seed 'em when I was out gittin' me a deer couple a days ago. But they never seen me. No sir, I'm too slick for that."

Hawke stood silent a moment, thinking swiftly. "Jed, I've got to save time. Will you take me up there to where you saw those fellows in the canyon?"

Jed nodded his head vigorously. "Dang right! Wait'll I get my gun."

As the two traveled, Hawke's brain was busy. The trail was growing hot, he knew it. From what Jed said, the camp in Granite Canyon was not more than eighteen miles from the scene of the train robbery, so situated that anyone could ride to it from Ute Cañon without danger of being seen by any human being. In less than two hours, Hawke and Dinkle reached the northern rim of Granite Canyon.

They paused in the cover of scrubby cedar growing on the rim, and looked squarely down on the camp of the two men Dinkle had seen there. The camp was not more than a hundred feet below them. A river rushed through the narrow gorge of the canyon, making so much noise that all lesser sounds were drowned. It was impossible to hear anything being said by the men, but

Hawke and Dinkle had a good view of them. The two fellows had pitched a dingy tent near a huge yellow pine. The men were seated in front of it, smoking and talking. One was a heavy-set man with brown hair and beard. Hawke had never seen him before.

But as his eyes focussed on the second man, they went hard as black flint. The second man was very nearly Hawke's own height and build. There was a strong similarity in his face to Hawke's. His hair was heavy, black and curly. Hawke said under his breath: "Cheyenne Slim! I thought so. But how in hell he ever followed me to the cove—"

"What's that? You know one of 'em?" Jed interrupted.

"Rather. That slim bean pole is Cheyenne Slim. You can't see it from here, but on his temple there's a long scar running up into his hair. That's my brand. I had to leave Wyoming damned suddenly for the pleasure of slapping it onto that crook. They'd have sent me up for 'assault with intent to kill.' Damn him, I wish I had killed him. Well, never too late to mend. Jed, beat it back to your cabin. I've business here. I'll be back—when I can."

If Jed's mind had been clearer he might have argued. But what little wits he had were easily dominated by Hawke Travis. He returned to his cabin.

• • •

Early this same morning, the morning after Hawke's escape from the jail, Anderson gathered up a posse in town. Among those present at Hawke's preliminary hearing was a stocky, bull-shouldered man with blue eyes and sandy hair. He had been an interested spectator and listener. He was prominently present when Sheriff Anderson was organizing his posse to pursue the escaped prisoner. When Anderson swore in the new members of the posse, the stocky man deliberately stepped up and raised his hand with the rest. Anderson shot him a sharp glance.

"You're a stranger, but I need all the men I can get. What's your name and business?"

"Jeff Preston, sheriff. I'm looking for tie timber for the D. & R. G. Railroad."

"Got a horse and gun?"

"Horse at the corral. Gun in my room at the hotel. I'll be with you in two shakes."

He rode with Anderson, one of the party of six that took the road for the cove. The other members of the posse scattered to ride in other directions. At the Cross ranch they were joined by old Buck. Anderson asked for Bill and Jerome. Cross said Bill had been up all night playing poker and had come home drunk. He was sleeping it off. Jerome had gone up the valley to try to find Hawke's trail. Buck joined the posse and they rode on. When they reached the cove they found Jerry on the porch and Sally standing in the yard with a broom in her hand.

"Which way did he go?" Anderson demanded.

"Find out!" Sally retorted and turned her back on him. Anderson scowled and ordered the posse on. After they had gone, the girl turned to Jerry.

"If we only knew where he was, to warn him."

"I'll bet a hat Jed knows," Jerry answered quickly. "We'll get the horses and ride for Jed's place."

Sally wanted to know who Jed was, and Jerry explained that he was the queer old coot living above the wash. The girl and the boy saddled the horses and rode for Jed's cabin. They swung around in an arc to avoid running into the posse. Within a quarter mile of the cabin, they dismounted, tethered the horses, and walked to an eminence from which they could see Dinkle's dwelling. The sheriff was standing in Dinkle's doorway looking about. From behind Jerry a querulous voice demanded:

"What yuh spyin' on my cabin for?"

Jerry whirled to face Dinkle. He introduced Sally, and explained that they had come to warn Travis, and asked if Dinkle knew where he was.

"He's up in Granite Canyon, keepin' cases on a couple of fellas camped there. I been hangin' around, expectin' to see the sheriff show up. And I been stayin' out of sight so he couldn't ask me no questions." His wits weren't all gone. He agreed with alacrity to lead them to the place where he had left Hawke. Dinkle had no horse, and Sally told him sharply to slip down and take the horse the sheriff had tethered in the brush beyond the cabin. Evidently Anderson intended waiting a while, determined to see Dinkle. It took Dinkle over a half hour to get the sheriff's horse, but he did it, and all three of them rode for Granite Canyon.

Meanwhile, Hawke had been keeping close watch from the rim of the canyon. The two men below seemed uneasy, and evidently were waiting for someone. Hawke was impatient to move down into the canyon and get the drop on them, but it was folly to try it until dusk fell. Just before sundown, Boone Trench and Bill Cross came riding up through the canyon at terrific speed. They drew their panting horses to a staggering halt, flung out of their saddles, and stood talking excitedly to the other two men. Boone Trench seemed most excited. He gesticulated several times, pointing at the main range of the Rockies to the west. The burly fellow with the brown beard was the only one who did not seem at all perturbed. Hawke judged that Trench was urging them to make a hurried departure.

It began to grow dusk, and the men were still arguing. Hawke decided that it was dark enough to slip down into the canyon. He rose, backed, and turned east along the rim. He found a place fairly easy of access, made his way down until he was as near as he dared go till it got darker. He paused behind a huge boulder and stood watching the four. The men had built a campfire, and were standing around it. He could hear their voices now, heated and angry, but the roar of the river drowned their words. Someone slipped up behind him and struck him a crashing blow on the back of the head. He never knew what hit him, a gun barrel maybe, or a rock. He went down and out.

When Anderson remained at Dinkle's cabin searching for some sign of Hawke's having passed, Preston slipped away from the rest of the posse and went on. He rode up a hogback leading to the rim of the mesa. He paused there, dismounted, and took a pair of powerful binoculars out of his pocket. Carefully he searched the regions to the east. He saw Trench and Cross riding at top speed for Granite Canyon, put his glasses back in his pocket, remounted his horse and followed them. Before he reached the canyon, he came across Jerry and Sally. He halted and surveyed them in surprise.

"Well, what are you doing away out here, miss? Who are you and the boy?"

"I might ask the same question," Sally returned coolly.

"My name's Preston. I'm here on business. Did you see a couple of men go by here lately?"

"We saw Boone Trench and Bill Cross, if you know who they are. We hid in the brush so they wouldn't see us."

Preston nodded, as though he were satisfied. "Come to warn Travis?" He guessed shrewdly. He smiled at the flare in the girl's eyes. "That's all right. Do you know Jed Dinkle?"

"Yes. Of course. He's here with us. He's back in the trees with the horses. We were waiting for Trench and Cross to get well out of the way before we rode on. You haven't said what you're doing here."

Preston smiled dryly. "I'm one of the posse. You'd better ride over to Dinkle's place for the night, all three of you. Granite Canyon is liable to be a hot place before morning. No place for a boy and a girl."

Sally had stiffened, a look of panic on her face, when Preston said he was one of the posse. "We're not going back. We'll beat you! We know where Travis is. You don't."

"I think I can find him." Preston's face grew grave. "Better listen to me. And—you might trust me. I'll warn Travis. That's what I'm here for. You go on back." And not waiting for any further arguments, he rode on. He hadn't gone far when Sally, Jerry and Jed came riding after him. It was now growing dusk, and they were nearing the canyon. With a resigned look on his face, Preston stopped to wait for them. They reached the canyon about a hundred yards below the camp of the men. Against the other wall of the canyon, the reflection of a fire showed in the gathering shadows. Preston nodded toward it.

"Apparently, they think they're safe. At that, the fire wouldn't show from any other direction. Now listen. Whatever you do, if you have any regard for the life of Hawke Travis, for God's sake do what I tell you to. Stay right here, while I sneak up there and see what they're doing."

With a long look into his face, Sally gave her word. The man who pretended to be a timber scout disappeared into the gathering night.

Hawke Travis returned to consciousness to find himself under a tree in the bandit camp. He lay motionless, eyes closed, listening for a moment, then opened his eyes barely enough to see through slits in his lids. The men had built a fire. Cheyenne Slim and Bill Cross were frying bacon at the fire, and getting a meal between them. Boone Trench and the brown-bearded man were squatting on their heels on the ground. Standing facing them was the man who had struck Hawke on the head, Jerome Cross. To cover quickly what Hawke later learned, this is what had happened. Bill Cross and Boone Trench had become highly alarmed when they learned that the posse was trailing Hawke Travis to Granite Canyon, where Cheyenne Slim and the bearded man were camped. Bill and Trench had ridden hastily to carry warning. Jerome had followed to try to keep Travis from getting the drop on the others. When Travis came back to consciousness, Bill Cross was talking.

"Fill him full of lead and throw him in the river."

The brown-bearded man objected violently. "Hell, that won't do at all. We've got to put him out so that it'll look like an accident. You have some fool ideas, like urging me and Slim to get out of here in daylight. That was a bright idea, I don't think! We might run into some of the posse, or get spotted. The only safe thing to do is get away after dark, and we're doing it pronto. You guys are safe. Nobody's got a damn thing on you. But we've got to beat it."

"Well, what are you going to do with him?"

"Easy. You wait and see."

They had left Hawke unbound, at which he had been surprised and puzzled when his head cleared and he realized it. There must be some good reason for it. The bearded man walked over to him, drew back a foot and kicked him in the ribs, evidently to make sure that he was still unconscious. Hawke leaped to his feet, a rock in his right hand, determined to fight to the last ditch. He crashed the rock squarely into the bearded man's face. The fellow grunted and went to his back. Hawke whirled, to dart away, but Cross thrust out a leg and tripped him. The next instant three of them were on top of him. Cross struck him over the head with a gun barrel, and Cheyenne Slim kicked him in the pit of the stomach. He lay gasping, two-thirds unconscious, as the bearded man sprang to his feet and joined Cross, his mouth cut, his nose bleeding, his face convulsed with fury.

"You, Bill and Slim, grab his feet. Get him by the shoulders, Trench. Carry him over there to the rim and throw him in the river. It's curtains for him, and no kick-back on us."

Hawke felt himself lifted, borne at a run for several yards, swung out and dropped. He felt himself falling, falling at sickening speed into the rushing stream.

As Preston came into sight of the campfire, Jerome Cross was standing in the glow of it, watching the three beyond him. The bearded man stood by him, a handkerchief thrust to his face. Just as Preston came into sight, he saw Trench and the other two heave Hawke into the river. He shuddered. Nothing could save the man now. The stream was murderous, full of swift currents, huge boulders and sink holes. It would be a miracle even if his dead body were ever found.

As Hawke dropped into the gorge, he thought he heard the crack of a gun. He couldn't be sure. He tried to clear his thought as he swooped downward, toward the water that rushed like a millrace, praying desperately that he would not strike on a boulder. He struck the water feet first, squarely between two boulders. He felt himself scrape against them as he went down. He bounded up to the surface, caught in the vicious current, rolling over and over. The chill of the icy water cleared his head, and though it ached violently, he kept his senses and fought the current with all the strength he had. Badly battered and nearly exhausted, he reached a place where the river widened and was less turbulent. It was deeper also, and he floated with the current, barely able to keep his head above the water.

In mid channel he struck against a rough boulder. It had a flat place on one side, and he managed to cling to it, his teeth chattering with a deadly chill. He squinted across at the shore, a dim blot against the black water. To swim to either shore wasn't a great task, the distance was not far. But he knew he could never make it. He was too nearly gone. He hadn't even strength left to cling to the boulder for more than a few short moments. The current tore at him. In no time at all it would pull him loose and suck him under. When it did that, he was gone. He stared at the bank to the left. It was a little more clearly to be seen. What faint light came from the sky was shed upon it. Trees and boulders there appeared distinct from the other objects as slightly more defined blots of blackness. As he stared, one of the black blots moved. It might be a wild animal

It might be a horse belonging to some member of the posse. It might be one of the posse, who would shoot at the first intimation of his presence. It might be anything.

He had nothing to lose. He exerted his last strength, and raised his voice. "Is there anybody over there?"

The river made an awful racket, but his voice was sharp with the agony of despair. It carried clearly. There was a moment's silence, and above the roar of the water he heard a cry in answer, as agonized as his own.

"Hawke! Hawke! Is that you? Where are you?"

Hawke shook his reeling head. That must be part of the nightmare. It sounded like the voice of Sally O'Brien. No doubt it was all a nightmare, and he was in reality swirling down the river, dreaming some wild thing like this in his last moment of consciousness near the end. Other nightmarish fancies, more voices from the bank.

"It came from the river, Sally. I tell you, he's in the river."

"In the river? Good God, Jerry, no!"

"He is too. We've got to get him."

More blots moving on the bank. Coming toward the river. One blot moving into the river toward him. Sally O'Brien, not five feet away, fighting the current, reaching out a hand.

"Jerry's got a rope tied around me, Hawke; got the other end tied to a tree. The current can't get us. Let go of the rock, and hold on to me."

More nightmares. He and the girl, clinging to each other desperately, fighting their way against the current, pulling themselves along the rope, reaching the shore and staggering out upon it. To find Jerry busily fanning into flame a fire he had built. No, it wasn't any nightmare. It was actuality. Shortly the fire was roaring, and he and Sally were close to it, absorbing the warmth, their wet clothes steaming. Hawke suddenly became aware that he was lying on his back with his head in Sally's lap, that her arms were around him, and that she was sobbing convulsively.

"Don't," he said harshly. "I've been a crook, a bandit, a killer, a professional gambler, everything bad that a man can be. Don't shed any tears for me."

The girl's arm tightened about his head. She choked back her sobs. "Do you think that matters? Hawke, regeneration has a price. You've paid it. Only one thing matters. If you care."

And Hawke Travis, who didn't believe in God, or a protecting Providence, who didn't believe in much of anything, turned his dark face against her arm. He said: "God knows I do. If it weren't for you I'd have gone down. There's not much left of me, but such as it is, you can have it."

From the canyon above there came a fusillade of shots, shots that barked above the roar of the river. The three at the fire listened. They heard faint shouts, other shots, then only the roar of the river. A few moments later, into the glow of the campfire walked Jeff Preston, Jed Dinkle at his heels. Preston stopped short as he saw Travis lying on the ground, his head on the girl's knee. His eyes widened and his jaw sagged.

"You?" he gasped. "Before God, I never expected to see you again."

"I never thought you would myself a few minutes ago. I guess the game's up. I believe I've seen you before."

Preston smiled. "I reckon you have, Travis. I was at your trial, though you didn't see me then. Yes, I guess the game's up." His eyes flicked at the girl, significantly. "You'll be playing a different one from now on. Come to think of it, I don't believe you ever did see me before. Don't believe I know you. If you've got any fool idea that I'm on your trail for any old scores, forget it. I'm special agent for the D. & R. G. I came up here after the bandits that held up the train. I had an idea Trench was the leader of the gang. You see, this goes back into history. Years ago, before you first located in the cove, the westbound passenger was looted on the Pass. We were certain Boone and his crowd did that little job. In the express car was a shipment of bricks from the mills at Telluride and Ouray. Boone's pal was killed on Pack Creek. Boone was seen crossing Little River the next day, heading for Brown's park. Still later, his riding horse and pack horse were found near the place you call the cove.

"We traced him from there to Denver, and on to Wyoming. We found him in the Laramie pen where he'd been sent for a stick-up. He had four gold bricks worth about eight thousand dollars apiece; they weren't found. I've been tailing him ever since he got out of Laramie, waiting for him to dig up those bricks. But he was too smart— until he made such a grandstand play to chase you out of the cove. Then I got wise. He planted those bricks under that big piñon in your front yard."

Hawke stared. "You mean to tell me I've been living right over some thirty thousand dollars worth of gold?"

Preston grinned. "I guess it was safe enough. I know it's safe enough now. I've already dug it up and cached it. When and how is nobody's business."

"But Cheyenne Slim, and Cross—"

"Dead. Dead as door nails," Preston returned curtly. "The lot of them. Layin' up there waitin' for the sheriff to come get 'em. I had the goods on 'em, and I took no chances. And I reckon you'd all better be getting home."

"Home," said Hawke Travis, "is a good word."

As they started on the trail back toward the cove, Hawke suddenly remembered that he had intended to return to Denver in the spring and trim the suckers. In the word Denver, he epitomized all the old lawlessness, all the wild ways of the other fork of the road, as he muttered to himself, "To hell with Denver!"

Not until then did he know that he had long since passed the parting of the ways. Regeneration. Sally had said it had a price, and that he had paid it. He didn't deceive himself. He knew he hadn't paid it all. It wasn't done that easily. There would be more, but he didn't care a great deal. He had made the turn. He would never again go back to the old ways. He never did. The years stretched on, and he went on, and up.

Today, a long, long life behind, he still travels the trail, alone. Sally is gone. What he had of her is a holy memory. He has worked out his own philosophy of life, groping toward the truth, come to see at last that truth alone can set a man free. He looks with grave eyes on life, black eyes beneath shaggy gray-white brows, still with some of the old devil in them, but eyes that have found a solid wisdom. All men, like him, progressing slowly but surely toward the light, draw from their lives something of understanding and tolerance for each other. He sees them that way.

He lives quietly. He is, to his neighbors, perhaps a lonely and rather strange character, but a man to be respected. He has a few pieces of property, and he lives on the income from them. He pays his bills and owes no man anything. He has a checking account in one of the large banks, good rating in the commercial agencies, and practically unlimited credit from the firms with which he deals. He lives quietly, yes, with a few books and magazines to keep him company. He has no telephone and no car. He doesn't want to be disturbed by the jangle of a bell. When he wants to talk to his friends, he goes to see them, and he walks. He is nearing eighty years of age, but he thinks nothing of walking from four to six miles to and from the house of a friend. He is, perhaps, happier than the ordinary man.

I don't know that he ever thinks of the end of life, the end that comes to us all some day. It is easily conceivable that for him the end is not yet for twenty or forty years. I don't suppose he ever thinks of a white stone that may one day be erected over the spot where he shall lie. No, I don't suppose he ever thinks about it, ever has thought about it. But if he did think of it and if he could have his way about what should be carved on that commemorating stone, I fancy he would choose, with his black eyes seeing back over a long stretch of time, that singing sentence all the world knows—

I KNEW THE WEST
WHEN IT WAS YOUNG.

Eli(za) Colter was born in Portland, Oregon. At the age of thirteen she was afflicted for a time by blindness, an experience that taught her to 'drill out' her own education for the remainder of her life. Although her first story was published under a *nom de plume* in 1918, she felt her career as a professional really began when she sold her first story to *Black Mask Magazine* in 1922. Her style clearly indicates a penchant for what is termed the 'hard-boiled school' in stories that display a gritty, tough, violent world. Sometimes there are episodes that become littered with bodies. Over the course of a career that spanned nearly four decades, Colter wrote more than 300 stories and serials, mostly Western fiction. She appeared regularly in thirty-seven different magazines, including slick publications like *Liberty*, and was showcased on the covers of Fiction House's *Lariat Story Magazine* along with the like of Walt Coburn. She published seven hardcover Western novels. Colter was particularly adept at crafting complex and intricate plots set against traditional Western storylines of her day-range wars, cattlemen vs. homesteaders, and switched identities. Yet, no matter what the plot, she somehow always managed to include the unexpected and unconventional, as she did in her best novels, such as *Outcast of Lazy S* (1933) or *Cañon Rattlers* (1939).